MW01490775

To: Laura

Always Focus on the good Stuff!

WHERE GRANDMA KEEPS THE GOOD STUFF

Deana Luna

Where Grandma Keeps the Good Stuff

Deanna Turner

WHERE GRANDMA KEEPS THE GOOD STUFF

Some parts of this book have been fictionalized in varying degrees, for various purposes.

ISBN: 9798877668935

To Christopher,

The love of my life, my biggest supporter, my top shelf. I love you endlessly.

Chapter One

Gabby took a deep breath and looked around, taking in the ambiance. There was too much light pollution to enjoy the night sky, but the hanging bistro lights around their cozy table for two and the light breeze gave it a dreamy aura. The patio was packed with people, but Gabby didn't notice. She was only focused on being present with Joe, and he made her feel like the only girl in the world.

Gabby sipped her rosé as the waiter brought over olive garlic focaccia and whipped feta. It was their third dinner date, and Joe had made coveted reservations for the patio at Girl and the Goat. The popular Chicago West Loop restaurant was usually booked for months in advance, and Gabby, a self-proclaimed "foodie," had been dying to try it out. Plus, it was her twenty-fourth birthday.

"You look so beautiful tonight. Happy birthday, baby," Joe said as he slid a petite, blue box with a white satin ribbon across the table to Gabby.

He smiled his beautiful lopsided smile with perfect white teeth. She felt like his eyes bored deep into her soul as he looked at her across the table.

Gabby's heart fluttered as she picked up the familiar-looking blue box. She untied the ribbon slowly and opened the gift to find a blueberry sapphire and nude diamond flower ring set in rose gold.

"Oh Joe, it's stunning! Thank you so much. I love it," she said as she leaned over the table and kissed him. Joe's lips were soft, and Gabby felt a hint of stubble on his chiseled face.

She slipped the ring onto her pointer finger. Sapphires were her birthstone and her favorite. It was a perfect birthday present and made her feel adored. Joe always had a way of making her feel special.

They had been dating for a few months, and he treated her like a queen. Joe took her to some of Chicago's best restaurants and bought her jewelry. He was in investment banking and drove a BMW.

He had a crooked smile, deep brown eyes, and dark, nearly black hair, with just a hint of gray. Joe was fifteen years older than Gabby, but that was a non-issue for her. He was much more mature than the men she usually dated and looked seductive and sophisticated in his gray suit with a black button-down shirt.

Gabby also felt particularly sexy in her light brown leather mini-skirt, tight black turtleneck top, and tall black boots. Her friend, Jules, called them her "hooker boots." Her hair hung in waves just over her shoulders. Since things had been going so well, Gabby was hoping tonight was going to be the night she and Joe would be intimate for the first time.

Joe put down his old-fashioned and reached across the table to hold Gabby's hand. As he fiddled with Gabby's new ring he said, "I was thinking … maybe I could finally see your place tonight … stay over."

Before Gabby could answer, commotion broke through her dream-like state induced by the rosé, Joe's husky voice, and the magic of the evening. Four women barged through the patio and approached their table. One of the women, a tall, slim blonde, started yelling. Her entourage surrounded her on all points.

"What are you doing? Who *IS* this?!"

Joe dropped Gabby's hand like she was on fire. "I'm just having dinner with a friend."

"A friend?" She turned her attention to Gabby. "I am his wife! Did you know he's married? Did you know he has kids?"

Gabby realized the hysterical blonde was now screaming and directing more questions her way. Stunned, Gabby quickly gathered her phone, purse, and black leather jacket, then abruptly left the restaurant. She rushed out embarrassed, fully aware of the people staring at her and the commotion erupting behind her.

Gabby stood outside on the sidewalk of Randolph Street trying to decide how she was going to get home. Obviously, that would not be happening via Joe Gallant and his BMW.

Randolph Street was considered "restaurant row," and it was packed with people coming and going to dinner. Gabby kept looking over her shoulder, expecting Joe's wife to appear with the

"Sisterhood of the Traveling Mom Jeans" swinging their Gucci totes that doubled as diaper bags.

She finally decided to get an Uber, since it would probably be the quickest way to get back to her River North apartment from the West Loop. While she waited for her ride, Gabby decided to text her best friend, Julia Savage, aka Jules to most.

G: *You are not going to believe what just happened.*

J: *Why are you texting me on your sexy night out with Mr. Joe?*

G: *Tonight was a disaster. Couldn't make this shit up if I tried.*

J: *Girl noooo!! WTF happened?!*

Jules was very outgoing and balanced the mostly introverted Gabby, who personally felt that she was not the type of girl that guys typically gravitated toward in the real world. Not like Jules, who was petite and blonde with big boobs. Gabby was average height, had long, brown wavy hair, and green eyes. She was not chubby but not thin and had a big heart and a smile that lit up any room.

It took Gabby many years to learn to be comfortable in her own skin. Before Joe, Gabby's only serious relationship was with her high school boyfriend, Jake, and even that did not come easily. They grew up next to each other but as they got older and developed different interests they drifted apart. When Gabby had to interview Jake for the homecoming football game, she was incredibly nervous because it had been so long since they had an actual conversation. He was a linebacker. She was a nerdy journalism student. Their relationship defied high school standards. And when they both went off to college and long distance didn't pan out, it left Gabby heartbroken.

G: *He is MARRIED! His wife and her entire entourage showed up at dinner! I was mortified.*

J: *If you didn't have bad luck, you would have no luck. I'm so sorry, friend.*

G: *I should be done with trying to find "love" right now. I can't even process what just happened. Maybe it's time to focus on Gabby. My Uber is here. Talk tomorrow.*

Chapter Two

Gabby walked into her modest apartment in the River North neighborhood and threw her keys and purse onto the small white table near the front door. She looked into the gold oval mirror that hung above the table and turned her head from side to side. She leaned in closer and really looked into her own eyes. They were a darker shade of green at the moment due to the tears Gabby shed on the ride home.

I am smart. I am cute. I deserve love and companionship. And gosh darn it, people like me. Gabby laughed out loud. She was raised on SNL and sarcasm.

Finding humor in things was a survival skill for her. She was quiet and shy in high school, which was mistaken for bitchiness before "resting bitch face" was even a thing. As a result, Gabby had a hard time making friends outside of journalism. And when she started dating Jake, the mean girls did not like that one bit. It was not an easy time for her.

She hadn't made it far through the door before her most loyal of friends, her cat Bartleby, voiced his annoyances with her. Gabby scooped up Bartleby and nuzzled his face and neck while she walked into her kitchen and poured herself a glass of wine.

"You are the king of the jungle, Mr. B. And I should have known that guy was too good to be true. Happy birthday to me," Gabby said as she raised her glass in Bartleby's direction.

Many of Gabby's friends had gotten married or started families, and the gap between those friendships had widened. Perpetually single and career-oriented Gabby was feeling a bit lonely. So, she signed up for a casual dating app called Match-Up. That is where she met the aforementioned Joe Gallant.

She wandered into her living room with Bartleby, then sat down on the chaise part of her sectional couch and tried to mentally forget about the evening. Gabby had just reclined onto the couch and got comfortable when her stomach growled.

Oh yeah, got screwed out of my birthday dinner! she thought and frowned. *I was so excited about that restaurant, too! And Joe… my ring… it was not supposed to be like this.*

She wandered back into the kitchen to find something to eat. *I really need to get to the grocery store,* Gabby thought as she rummaged through her fridge. *Guess I have been eating out a lot lately.* She dumped out the last of her wine and made herself a peanut butter sandwich with a tall glass of milk. It was just enough to tide her over until morning.

Gabby sat down on her couch with her dinner and turned on the TV. The familiar song "I'll be there for you…" was playing. As she settled in with her sandwich and a re-run of her favorite show, *Friends*, her phone dinged.

YOU HAVE A MATCH!

"Ugh ... too soon," Gabby informed Bartleby as she put her phone on "do not disturb." *Just one episode,* she told herself.

Ironically, the episode was called "The One with Ross's Inappropriate Song" and was about Ross dating a much younger student of his who he later finds out has a boyfriend.

After the show was over, Gabby decided to call it a night and get ready for bed. She had an early day and would need at least two cups of coffee before she encountered Jules, the glorious morning person that she was. She hated mornings and hated Monday mornings even more. *What I wouldn't give to have Jules's energy and first light attitude,* Gabby thought.

Despite their literal night and day personalities, Jules had become one of her closest friends in the city. They met their first week at the United Center where they both worked as premium sales account executives for the Chicago Bulls and Chicago Blackhawks. Gabby was shy and quiet. Jules was loud and boisterous. But they clicked. The two of them navigated their new jobs together and quickly built a bond.

"Hello! I'm Julia, but most people call me Jules."

"Hello, I'm Gabriella. Only my mom calls me that, and it's usually if she's annoyed with me. You can call me Gabby."

"You new here too?" Jules asked her.

"Straight from Northwestern University! Go Cats! *Meow*," Gabby laughed, then shook her head. "I have no idea why I said that."

"Hail to Purple! Hail to White! Hail to thee, Northwestern!" Jules responded in a sing-songy voice.

"You went to Northwestern too??" Gabby squealed. "Oh my god. Did we just become best friends?"

They both cracked up and the rest, as they say, is history.

Jules had a knack for pulling Gabby out of her shell. Her personality was enigmatic. Gabby loved to have fun and laugh but was much more reserved than her bestie. She always felt that was a negative when it came to meeting guys organically.

In addition to having a very small inner circle, Gabby had grown accustomed to living alone and preferred not having roommates. Even in her final years as an economics major at Northwestern University, she chose to live in a single room at

Goodrich House. If there was somewhere in between introvert and extrovert, it had Gabby written all over it. A creature of habit – homebody when she wanted to be – she also enjoyed traveling and experiencing new things. She loved to be home alone until she didn't. When Gabby felt that way, she wandered over to the museum campus and explored the many exhibits, the aquarium, or the planetarium.

Her apartment reflected her personality. Looking around, aside from Bartleby, you would find lots of cozy blankets and pillows, a few plants she managed to keep alive, and several bookshelves overflowing with books of different genres and trinkets from her travels.

Aside from her books, her favorite thing about her apartment was her bed. It was one of those Purple mattresses and literally felt like she was sleeping on a cloud. It was on the expensive side and her first big purchase when she got her first "big girl job," as Jules called it.

After Gabby washed her face, she put on her most comfortable, cozy pjs, then pulled her duvet close to her chin as Bartleby folded himself next to her legs.

It was autumn in the city, and Chicago's weather was really starting to change to her favorite time of the year. Gabby put on her sleep mask with built in speakers and listened to her favorite *Get Sleepy* podcast. The narrator was talking about a cozy and rainy autumn day. The story was full of beautiful descriptions of baked apples, walks along paths of crunchy fallen leaves, pumpkin spice, and cups of tea. It wasn't long before Gabby forgot about her miserable birthday and was completely lulled to sleep.

Chapter Three

Gabby's phone rang as she pulled into a parking spot in the employee lot of the United Center. She put her red Chevy Equinox into park and picked up her phone.

"Hey, Mom."

"Gabriella, how was your birthday dinner last night? Also, are you coming home this weekend? We have gifts for you and would like to celebrate."

"Long story, Mom. Last night was … eventful. And yes, I planned on coming home. I miss you guys and I could use a home-cooked meal and some family time. I need to ask Jules to check in on Bartleby for me."

"Wonderful. Guess who I saw at Woodman's a couple days ago? Jakey's mom! She said Jakey is working in the city too and asked about you. He's going to be in Buffalo Grove this weekend. Maybe he can come over and celebrate with us."

Gabby sighed. Jacob Rogers was Gabby's high school boyfriend both her junior and senior year. And Gabby's parents just loved him. And evidently still did.

"Gosh, I haven't talked to Jake in a really long time. Okay Mom, I have to get going and get to work. I will call Friday when I am on my way."

Gabby pulled down her visor and double-checked her modest makeup. She was not one to go overboard with any of it and preferred a natural look. She mostly only wore mascara, some concealer where needed, and lip gloss. That day, Gabby had her hair pulled back into a ponytail. She wore black slacks that were on the skinny side with some black ankle booties and a cream-colored blouse that billowed in the sleeves and had a slight "v" in the front. She wasn't much for fashion, either. Gabby wasn't raised with a material mindset. She wasn't much of a "girly-girl" and loved sports. But she also liked to be pampered and enjoyed the occasional spa day.

Gabby had lived in Buffalo Grove, a suburb of Chicago, most of her life. She was the only child to two educators, Mark and Veronica Price. They had a modest home in a middle-class neighborhood: not rich, not poor. Just right. Gabby never went without because her parents worked hard to provide her with a good life and college education.

She spent her weekends growing up at the library, at art fairs, at farmer's markets, and traveling every summer. Looking back, it felt very organic and natural to her. She never felt the need for material things. And Gabby was a saver. She preferred to spend her extra money and time on experiences.

Gabby was looking forward to returning to her childhood home and connecting with the high school friends she kept in touch with. There were only a handful she still connected with and talked to regularly. It was the same small group she spent free time with during high school.

At Northwestern, Gabby didn't make too many friends. She immersed herself in studying and avoided the party scene. She dated here and there but as far as boyfriends go, she was never serious about anyone in college. In fact, she wasn't serious about anyone except for Jake until she met Joe Gallant. She really let her guard down and went all in. And we all know how that ended.

Gabby was only sitting in her cubicle for what felt like two seconds when she felt her chair spin around and saw Jules standing there with two lattes in her hands.

"Spill the tea," she said as she handed Gabby her coffee.

Gabby groaned as rehashing the previous night was not at the top of her morning agenda. However, Jules was like a dog with a bone when she wanted information. So, she obliged her.

"Boy, I would love to give him the what-for. What a douche," Jules said after Gabby finished her recap. "I'm so sorry. I know how much you were looking forward to that dinner."

"It was my birthday. The setting was romantic. Joe looked great. His wife and her friends storming in was so humiliating. Don't get me wrong; I feel bad for her. But I also feel bad for myself. You know? It's going to take me awhile to get over this. I really thought we had potential." Gabby frowned. "Maybe it's time for me to be selfish. I'll still date around, but I am not getting serious with anyone anytime soon. I'm not putting my heart out there."

"I am here for it all and love that for you," Jules replied. "By the way, we have a team meeting in ten minutes."

Jules and Gabby sat side by side in the sales team conference room. Gabby tapped her pen against her notebook while she stared out the window. She watched the leaves floating by as they fell off the trees and the wind swept them away. Thoughts swirled around in her mind like an unstoppable tornado.

How could I have been so naïve? How could I have let my guard down enough to be duped by a married guy? Think about it, Gabby. You had never been to his place. You only saw him during the day. He only messaged you through the dating app. Oh my god, I was his side chick!!

"Gabby, you with us?" her boss, Mack, asked.

Gabby felt a sharp kick to the back of her chair legs as she snapped back into focus. *Always the tactful one, Jules.*

"Yes, sorry!" Gabby said as her face flushed. She felt a bit embarrassed. *I cannot believe I am letting that jack wagon take up any more of my head space. Don't spiral, Price! He's not worth it.*

"As we were saying, the Blackhawks are kicking off their home opener next week, and we will have a buffet set up in the sales suite for the sales team. Take the week to check in on your clients and make sure your suites are full. We look forward to another successful year for the United Center."

As they walked back to their cubicles, Jules teased Gabby, "What are your plans this weekend? Got any hot dates? Too soon?"

Gabby groaned and then said, "Oh my god, I forgot to ask you! Could you check in on Bartleby? I am going to Buffalo Grove this weekend to see my parents and celebrate my birthday. Why not trade in some city stress for some suburban stress and incessant parental interrogation of my love life? My mom will probably have my hope chest open with china and Jakey prom pictures on display. Maybe I should just cancel … No, I can't. I just hung up with my mom before work."

"I hate to interrupt your riveting diatribe, but yes, I can check on Bartleby for you. Just bring me back some Myrtles from Long Grove."

Gabby worked at Long Grove when she was in high school. Long Grove Confectionary Co. was a local chocolate shop in Buffalo Grove. Their signature dessert was called "The Myrtle:" fresh, salted, roasted pecans covered with buttery caramel and smothered in rich chocolate. It was a cute, homey chocolate shop and factory with a storefront that looked like an old red schoolhouse.

"Yeah, yeah. Myrtles. You got it. I think you are getting the better end of the deal. Empty apartment, peace and quiet, chocolates, Bartleby …"

Jules shrugged and turned back to her computer while Gabby sat down at her workstation in the next cubicle. Jules had two roommates, and it was always constant chaos and partying at her place. Her two roommates were sorority sisters from college and, ironically, Jules was the most responsible member of that trio. Her sisters from Alpha Chi Omega were not quite as settled as Jules. While Jules liked to have a good time as much as the next person, she was the only one of the three with a steady job. The other two waitressed and modeled. And partied.

A few hours later, Gabby was reading through emails as a message popped up on her Teams messenger. Of course, it was Jules. Their cubicles were side by side, but they often messaged each other since they had very little privacy in their office area.

"Cafeteria or Billy Goat for lunch?"

Gabby stood and threw a wadded piece of paper at Jules' head. Jules opened the balled-up paper which read *Cafeteria!* Gabby sent Jules a subsequent message that said, *I have to finish up this email and I will meet you by the elevators.*

One of the many perks that came with working at the United Center was free daily meals in the cafeteria. It was a perk they liked to take advantage of often. Gabby definitely liked to save her money where she could.

"Billy Goat or cafeteria? Really? Did I mention one is F R E E?" Gabby said as they made their way to eat. "No more fancy lunches with Joe Gallant."

"We just gotta get you one of those *suite* sugar daddies so we can eat out whenever we want to again." Jules elbowed Gabby. "Pun intended."

"Hard pass. And hardly a requirement. Which doesn't matter now because I am not wasting my time. Ugh, did I mention the focaccia bread?" Gabby sighed. "I had been dying to get a table at that restaurant and didn't make it past the bread and a glass of rosé. You know what I ate for my birthday dinner? A peanut butter sandwich!"

"I love that the food was more important than the douchey guy and his wife and her entourage

crashing," Jules laughed and then changed her tone.
"Seriously though, are you okay?"

"As awful as I do feel about it all, I guess I
dodged a bullet. You see the picture of the ring I sent
you? Should I keep it? It just feels so weird now. It is
a beautiful ring. And he has given me earrings and
bracelets before. But never a ring. Rings just feel
more intimate to me. I left it in my jewelry box. Just
feels weird to wear it."

"I mean, keep it. Sell it. Wear it. Love it. You do
you, boo," Jules said. "Honestly, it was a gift, and if
you love it, just keep it. You have nothing to feel bad
about. Think of it as a parting gift."

Jules and Gabby grabbed trays and mused
over the cafeteria offerings. Gabby chose the three-
cheese mac and a Caesar salad. *Comfort food.*

"It's all about balance, you know. And you
know I can be bit of an emotional eater," Gabby said.

"And that's why I conned you into keeping a gym bag here at the office," Jules teased. "Balance, as you say."

"Yeah, yeah. We know you like to keep it *tight*," Gabby laughed.

The cafeteria was pretty crowded most days with people from all over the company. Gabby didn't know an eighth of the people she saw from day to day. They scanned the room and found a table for two near the food line. After they sat down with their trays, about five athletic-looking guys came through the doors and got in line.

"Yum. I will have me some of that for lunch." Jules wiggled her eyebrows.

"Try to control yourself. We are at work," Gabby snickered.

One of the guys made eye contact with Gabby and winked at her. He was tall and wore gym shorts and a tank top that showed off an athletic physique.

He had longish dark brown hair that fell near the nape

of his neck.

Jules broke Gabby's trance and said, "I wonder

where those hotties work."

"Who knows and who cares? I feel a bit

disgruntled and plan to be for some time," Gabby said

as she took a bite of her mac and cheese.

"That's fine. More for me!" Jules laughed.

Chapter Four

Gabby pulled into the driveway of her childhood home in the cul-de-sac of Aspen Court. The brick Tudor-style house always gave her English countryside cottage vibes and made her smile. It was a modest three-bedroom home with a beautiful stone fireplace near the arched front door.

She got out of her car, and as she grabbed her weekend bag from the backseat, she noticed the "For Sale" sign in the yard. *What the actual eff ...* Gabby slammed the car door and walked up the sidewalk, taking a deep breath as she entered the house.

"Mom! Dad!"

Gabby set her bag down in the foyer and walked into the kitchen. "Anyone here? Hello?!"

She peeked into her parents' shared office and then their bedroom. No Veronica or Mark but lots of empty moving boxes stacked along the walls of the office/library. Gabby then climbed the stairs to her top floor attic bedroom. It was not an attic in the traditional sense, but the bedroom encompassed the entire top floor of the house.

At one end there was a seat where she used to read all the time in the window that faced Jake's house. Sometimes she would see him waving at her from his bedroom out of the corner of her eye. Gabby would shake her book at him jokingly to let him know he was disturbing her precious reading time. At the other end was a vanity in front of another window, and along the wall between the two were shelves of books and a desk.

She sat down on her bed and looked around her favorite room. Her full-size bed still had tons of her favorite stuffed animals arranged on the pillows. She picked up a large stuffed dog that was in the middle of the bed. Jake had won her that dog during

Buffalo Grove Days, which was a local hometown fair. On the bulletin board above her desk were pinned pictures of her friends laughing, bowling, dancing, and graduating. She sighed and turned around where she noticed the folded-up boxes labeled GABBY leaning against the wall. Before she could process any emotion, she heard her mom call up from downstairs.

"Gabriella!! We're home! Are you here?"

Gabby made her way down the stairs. Along the wall of the staircase were pictures of her as a baby, kindergarten graduation, high school graduation, college graduation, family vacations, and many more special memories. Veronica and Mark were incredibly proud of Gabby and her accomplishments.

She rounded the corner and walked into the kitchen where her mom was setting down two pizza boxes and a cake on the white marble kitchen counter. She gave her mom and dad hugs, then sat down at their eat-in kitchen island.

"You two have something you forgot to share with me?"

Veronica Price shared a look with her husband, Mark. "Oh, honey. We were going to tell you, but everything happened so fast!"

"So fast you couldn't have sent a text message to say 'Oh, by the way, we have listed your childhood home for sale. Not sure if you have an opinion about that. Or if we even care.'"

"Oh Gabriella, don't be so dramatic! It hasn't even sold yet. But we have had lots of interest and wanted to talk to you about packing up some things this weekend. *In person.*"

"Well, I'm not going to lie. I do feel completely blindsided."

"And we feel terrible about that, honey. It was definitely not our intention. With us recently retired, and you all settled in the city, it really got us thinking about our future and what we want to do in this next phase of our lives."

"I understand. As much as I can, I guess. Still makes me a little sad."

"And we understand. But let's not be sad right now. We are celebrating! Come eat. You must be starving. We got Rosati's – your favorite!"

"Nothing like eating your feelings to take away the sting of losing a piece of your childhood."

But it did help. Her parents were talking about upcoming vacation plans as Gabby dug her fork into a nice slice of warm, gooey, Chicago-style deep dish pizza. The crispy crust had layers of meat and cheese, and on top of it all was a rich, savory marinara sauce. Rosati's was the best pizza joint in

Buffalo Grove. Jake worked there in high school and, of course, it was their go-to for takeout.

"We know how much you love lemon, so your birthday cake is lemon with lemon buttercream frosting. You ready for a piece?" Veronica asked her daughter.

"Yes, please." Gabby held out her plate for a slice. Food really was a source of comfort to her. The hot cheesy pizza and the sweet lemony cake filled up holes in Gabby's soul. Combined with being in her childhood home and the company and conversation with her parents, it was cathartic.

"Where will you live once the house sells?" Gabby asked her parents. "You know my apartment is only a one-bedroom," she joked.

Gabby's father said, "We actually are thinking about buying an RV and traveling around the country to start. There are a few places we haven't seen. And a few we would like to revisit."

"Well, that does sound exciting," Gabby mused. "And you two certainly deserve it."

"And you deserve this!" Gabby's mom pulled out a bag from behind her and set it in front of Gabby.

Gabby opened the bag to find Stephen King's newest book and a gift card to Lume Wellness Spa, which is in the city.

"Thank you so much! I could definitely use a spa day. And another Stephen King to add to my collection!" Gabby hugged her parents.

Gabby's dad wheeled over her other gift, brand new luggage. "For when you come visit," he said.

The luggage was bright orange and had a smaller suitcase inside and a carry-on inside of the smaller one. *Like little nesting dolls,* Gabby thought. The largest suitcase had a cupholder you could pull out. And a USB port. *In case I want to wheel around the airport with my Starbucks like a fancy jetsetter.*

"Get in line, Dad. I also have a trip to Paris I am saving up for. You sure the luggage isn't for packing up my stuff upstairs?" Gabby quipped.

"You did see the boxes with your name on them," her dad fired back and laughed.

"If I happen to see Jake this weekend, I am going to con him into helping me pack."

"Especially all those books," her mom said. "The thought of downsizing and getting rid of our clutter gives me heart palpitations."

"Can you get a custom RV with a library inside?" Gabby asked.

"But where will you sleep when you come visit?" her dad pondered.

"Valid point, Dad. Valid point."

Gabby was sitting on her parents' brick patio with a little fire burning and a glass of wine. It was late, and there was a chill in the air, but the sky was beautiful and bright with limitless stars. You could not see stars like this back in the city, and she would miss these views.

The suburbs weren't so bad in hindsight. She thought about the times growing up when she couldn't wait to get to the city and live there full time. It wasn't as glamorous as she envisioned it, but she was happy. Just a bit lonely as far as male companionship.

Gabby pulled the red and black buffalo check blanket tighter and breathed in the smoky scent of the fire and the crisp autumn air. She put her head back and looked up. *It's amazing how small you feel when*

you look at the vastness of the sky above. Like all the
BS of the previous week seem so insignificant, Gabby
thought. *If only it were that easy.*

"Hey, girl. Is there room for me under that
blanket?"

Gabby looked over and saw Jake standing on
the edge of the brick patio. She smiled big because
even though time had passed, he will always be "her
Jake." He had thick light brown hair that always fell
over one eye. Gabby used to love brushing it away so
she could look into those blue and sparkly bright eyes
of his. Jake had a very sexy smile and dimples that
made him look boyish. He was tall and, despite the
years, still had his football physique.

They didn't end their relationship on bad terms,
just bad circumstances due to distance. Jake went to
the University of Michigan in Ann Arbor, Michigan. It
was too much traveling back and forth to make it

work. Their breakup was like a one-two gut punch. She lost her boyfriend and best friend at the same time. Gabby's idea of healing was diving headfirst into school and staying laser focused.

She would never forget how nervous she was when they met. To her surprise, Jake was sweet and did not act like a stereotypical jock, which put her at ease. She was shocked when he asked her out on a date to the local movie theater. He was her first kiss, her first love, her first *everything.*

Gabby patted the seat next to her.

Jake sat down and gave Gabby a side hug. "It's been a minute. How are you? Your mom told my mom you were going to be home this weekend."

"Oh, I see. So, since you knew I was going to be home, you also made the trip?"

He was so easy to flirt with. It was familiar. Safe. And god, he smelled good. But he always did.

He always wore Curve cologne. It was his signature scent. She closed her eyes, and for a moment they were back in his car, at the prom, and snuggled on his basement couch watching a movie.

"Better make the time while you can," Gabby quipped. "I can't believe they are selling this place!"

"It's a bit surreal," Jake said. "You were my girl next door."

"Literally," Gabby laughed. "You got plans tomorrow? I could use some help packing up my entire childhood into some boxes."

"Of course. Anything for you." Jake gave Gabby a kiss on the cheek and stood. "Text me when you wake up. Number's the same."

With a wink and a wave, her first love disappeared into the shadows and through his own childhood backyard.

Chapter Five

Gabby's phone chimed as she fumbled around for it on her nightstand. Finally, she pulled her eye mask up onto her forehead so she could see better. It was Jules.

Fed Bartleby. Drank some wine. Ate your food. Stole your shit.

Gabby laughed as she heard a knock at her bedroom door.

"Gabby, it's your mom."

"Mom, just open the door!"

"I just like to give you your privacy. Dad and I are running into town to pick up some more boxes and tape from the hardware store. We are also going to meet Fred and Nancy at Prairie House for lunch. Do you want us to bring you some takeout?"

"How about you just text me when you're on your way back and I will let you know? Thanks, Mom."

After a few moments, Gabby heard the front door close, and she padded over to her little bathroom to start the shower. When Gabby started middle school, her dad remodeled a portion of her bedroom to give Gabby her own private bathroom. She truly felt so special that her dad did that for her. Mark Price wasn't the handiest of men, but he spent hours reading handyman books and made multiple trips back and forth to the hardware store to make that project happen for his little girl.

Her whole room and bathroom were white with accents and shades of green and blue. It kind of had a beachy theme. It was the most calming and beautiful space. She really needed to recreate some of it back at her apartment.

Need more Zen in my life. Scents. Calming hues, Gabby thought to herself while in the shower. *Home is my sanctuary.*

Gabby was not fully dressed as she pulled on a fresh t-shirt and started to towel dry her hair when she heard Jake call up from the bottom of the stairs.

"Yo! Gabs!"

"Getting dressed!" Gabby yelled back.

Before she got an answer, Jake was standing in her doorway with that goofy, lopsided smile. He was wearing basketball shorts, a Buffalo Grove Bison football sweatshirt, and a backward baseball cap.

"Memory is long and it's nothing I haven't seen before." Jake winked.

Gabby could see those sparkly bright blue eyes across the room, and her heart skipped a beat. Like no time had passed …

"Grab my leggings out of my bag and toss them over here. Don't try to distract me. We have a lot to pack up."

Jake did as he was told and then picked up the stuffed dog from her bed and held it up like he was making it speak. In his goofiest voice he said, "You mean to tell me you didn't take Mark Woofalo to your new place with you?"

Gabby laughed. "He did come to college with me. And he will be going home with me on Sunday. Along with all this other stuff," she gestured around the room. "I hope it all fits in my Equinox."

"Well, if not, I can make a special trip to your place and bring over what is left," Jake offered. He hugged the stuffed dog to his chest and looked around the room. "Man, so many memories … so many firsts … and lasts."

"Hey now. Don't be getting all mushy and sentimental on me. I need you to put your game face on. I don't intend on being stuck up here all day. I fully plan on whooping your ass later at Bowlero. That is, if you want to come along."

"Hell yeah," Jake said enthusiastically. "Logan text me earlier about going."

Bowlero was their local bowling alley which also had beer, wings, bumper cars, and an arcade. Many high school weekend nights were spent at that place with the gang, Addy, Lauren, and Maia, Gabby's journalism friends, and Logan, Will, and Travis. Those were Jake's football buddies. When Gabby and Jake started dating, their friend groups blended nicely for a group of writers and jocks.

Gabby, being the book nerd she was, read that the number eight was considered a symbol of balance, stability, and support in some cultures. From then on, their friend group was called the "Infinity Squad." Infinity since it's shaped like the number eight, and they all vowed to be a part of each other's lives beyond high school.

"Whoever packs up the most boxes – loser buys the first round," Gabby challenged Jake.

"I know your game, Price. Bring it!"

Gabby and Jake spent most of the morning packing up her room, laughing at old photos and reminiscing about growing up on their street. They were fortunate to have many kids their age to hang out with in the neighborhood. There were at least twenty of them all within a year or two of each other's ages. They played "Ghosts in the Graveyard" at one neighbor's house, had swim parties at another, watched movies and played video games in Jake's basement, rode their bikes all over, and Gabby's yard always had the pickup games whether it be baseball, kickball, soccer, or football. Her house had a big side yard that backed up to the woods, so there was a lot of room for all the sports.

Gabby started to get a little teary-eyed at all the memories.

"I really thought someday I would be bringing my kids to this house for the holidays. It's just so weird. I don't even know where my parents will end up. They plan on doing a bunch of traveling for a bit."

"Get over here. You look like you need a hug," Jake said.

Gabby snuggled in next to Jake on the bed and breathed in his fresh clean sweatshirt mixed with a hint of his cologne. He felt warm and safe as Jake wrapped his arms around Gabby and held her close. They laid there in silence for a few minutes. She could hear his heart beating as she laid her head on his chest.

Jake shifted a bit, so his face was closer to Gabby's. She reached up and brushed aside the hair that fell over one of his eyes. And before she could say a word, Jake's mouth was on hers. Familiar and safe was good. Gabby welcomed it.

I'm single. He's single. I think. Better put a pin in that one. And it's Jake. My Jake.

Chapter Six

Gabby, Jake, and the rest of the "Infinity Squad" took up two lanes at the bowling alley. No one was super great at bowling, but it didn't stop the bets and constant shit talking.

"Hey Logan!" Maia yelled. "You better pick up that split! Looks like your ex-girlfriend's teeth!"

Everyone laughed and groaned, and before Logan threw his ball, he casually reached into his pocket and pulled out his middle finger.

Addy had returned from the bar with a tray of shots and another round of Apple Orchard Hard Ciders. "Gather 'round Bison Bitches!! In honor of *moi*, I present the "red-headed slut.*"

She held up a shot made with cranberry juice, peach schnapps, and Jagermeister. It had a dark red tint to it and, of course, Addy had long, beautiful, curly red hair.

Before they took their shots, all four guys started loudly singing, *"Fight on you Bison, fight till the end, and we'll see you out on top all right! Hail to orange and blue and white, so bright for the victory we'll gain tonight. FIGHT!! FIGHT!! FIGHT!!"*

"Alright, guys," Lauren chimed in. "You cannot possibly be drunk enough to need to relive your football glory days."

"Have you seen Logan throw a bowling ball?" Maia joked.

"Keep it up, girl," Logan teased Maia. "You're up next Price!"

"Wait! Let's do our shots first," Travis said.

Will cleared his throat and lifted his shot in the air, "Here's to lying, cheating, stealing, and drinking... If you're going to lie, lie for a friend. If you're going to cheat, cheat death. TO THE INFINITY SQUAD!"

"TO THE INFINITY SQUAD!" everyone said in unison.

Gabby shuddered after she set down her shot glass. "I forgot you don't like Jager," Addy said to her.

"Or anything black licorice," Gabby responded.

"There are some things I forgot. Most I have remembered," Jake said as he intertwined his fingers with Gabby's. He leaned over and sweetly kissed her on the lips. "Like how those lips taste."

Maia and Lauren both exchanged some side-eye looks. When Gabby and Jake broke up, it was hard on the whole group as they felt like they had to choose sides. Fortunately, with the time that had passed, they all seemed to pick up where they left off.

Addy handed Logan a beer and said, "Looks like you could use this. Take the sting out of missing that split."

"It's okay, Logan. Split happens!" Maia laughed.

Logan walked over to Maia's seat and pretended to put her in a head lock.

Gabby hopped up to grab her drink, and Jake grabbed a handful of her butt. The flirting and sexual tension was off the charts.

And Gabby loved every minute of it.

As she waited for her ball to return, the song "Best Friend" by Saweetie came on. She started dancing in place and shaking her ass subtly to the beat. She looked over her shoulder to see Jake looking over his beer and watching her.

After Gabby took her turn, the girls gathered and sang, *"That's my best friend, she a real bad bitch, drive her own car, she don't need no Lyft."* They danced and sang while the guys took turns bowling.

Gabby started to walk back to her seat as Jake grabbed her hand and pulled her down onto his lap. She wrapped her arms around his neck and kissed him playfully as she whispered in his ear, "Are you trying to get me drunk? Because trust me, you don't need to."

"Another round," Jake laughed and swirled and pointed his finger in the air.

Lauren poked Gabby in the side and tipped her head back towards where Maia and Addy were standing. They walked over to a tall table that was behind the group and out of earshot.

"What's going on with you two?" Addy asked Gabby.

"You didn't say anything in the group text that us girls are in," Lauren added.

"I'm not sure I'm ready for 'Jabby' to be reinstated. Because if it falls apart again, who is left to pick up the pieces this time? We're all spread around right now," Maia said.

Gabby put her hands up, "Whoa whoa whoa. Jake and I only hung out today for the first time in a very long time. Nothing happened besides cuddling and kissing. I appreciate all your concerns. I promise I'm not looking to jump back into all that any time soon. And yes, let's lose the term, 'Jabby.' Makes him sound like a chump."

Just then, Will returned from the bar with another tray of shots. The girls were all laughing as they made their way back to wear the guys were sitting. This time the shots were vodka cranberry. As he handed them around, he said, "Hey, remember that time we were drinking in that field near Logan's house over summer break, and *someone* decided they needed Taco Bell? Like, right then?"

Maia coughed and tried to secretly point. "Gabby ..."

"In my defense, I was normally the designated driver and was quite the lightweight," Gabby retorted.

Lauren added, "So, we climbed into my old Monte Carlo, which of course was a two-door. And Miss Graceful Gabby fell into the backseat while trying to climb in."

Addy snorted while laughing, "And then we got to the drive through of Taco Bell, and she tried to lean forward from the back seat to place her order. But instead said, 'I'll take a Whopper. Whopper with cheese, please. We were dying."

"Wait, why don't I remember this story?" Jake asked.

"It was the first summer after our breakup. You had stayed in Michigan because you had that internship," Gabby said quietly.

"Shit. I'm sorry," Jake said.

"It's all good. In the past. To the Infinity Squad!"
Gabby said as she lifted her shot glass in the air.

"TO THE INFINITY SQUAD!"

Being with her friends and Jake was exactly
what she needed to press reset. It filled up her cup.
And a little of those holes in her soul.

Chapter Seven

Jake helped Gabby load the last of the boxes into her car and shut the hatch for her. Her car was packed to the brim with boxes from her room, along with her new luggage. Her dad lent her a four-wheeled trolley to use to unload her car when she got back to the city. *Thank god there is an elevator!*

Jake then leaned against the car, grabbed her hand, and pulled her closer to his body. "I had a great time with you yesterday." He smiled with his hands on Gabby's hips.

"Me too, Jake. We always seem to pick right up where we left off. Felt like old times with you and everyone," Gabby said. *But especially you.*

"Don't be a stranger." Jake pushed some hair behind Gabby's ear. "I know Chicago is a big city and all ..."

Gabby leaned in for a big hug and a quick kiss. "We will definitely hang out. Your office isn't too far from the United Center, right? We can have lunch at the Billy Goat."

"My girl next door to the big city girl."

"I'm still me … and you're still …you. Hey, I'm going to run inside to say bye to my parents and try to get back to the city before dark. It was good to see you. Thank you for helping me pack. And for the walk down memory lane."

"In more ways than one," Jake said with a wink.

Gabby gave him a playful punch in the arm before she walked into the house.

Gabby waited until she was on I-94 headed back to the city when she said, "Hey Siri, call Jules."

When Jules answered, Gabby said, "Hey girl hey. What are you up to?"

"Girl, I haven't moved off this couch. I am all about the sweats and HGTV today," Jules replied.

"You hungover? What did you do this weekend?" Gabby asked.

"I went to the Violet Hour with Marissa and Kelly last night. These guys were buying us drinks right and left. I had – I don't even know how many Paloma's but knew well enough to cut myself off and buddy system it the hell out of there before I ended up a *Dateline Special*."

Gabby laughed. Jules always made her laugh.

"I'm on my way back. You don't have to go check on Bartleby today."

"Uh, before we hang up. How was *your* weekend?"

"Well, the short of it – my parents are selling the house, I packed up my childhood bedroom, and I went bowling with my high school boyfriend and a bunch of our friends. There was a lot of flirting and sexual tension. We kissed, nothing more. Not to say that it couldn't have led to more."

"Well, that hiatus didn't last long. Girl, you should have led with that information!"

"I mean, it's not why I went home. Or what I intended to happen. Jake is just … Jake. It's hard to explain. I was so heartbroken when we broke up our freshman year of college. But he's single. I'm single. Honestly, it just felt good to be home and be around friends."

"Ouch."

"You know what I mean. Present company notwithstanding. My emotions were all over the map this weekend. I cried. I laughed. I got drunk. But Jake grounds me, if that makes sense. It's comfortable. Like an old sweatshirt."

"Wow. Sexy. Like an old sweatshirt," Jules laughed.

"Hardy har. Okay, I am going to hang up now. I will see you at work tomorrow."

"I want to see a picture of this *Jake* and hear more details in the morning. I'll bring the lattes, and you spill the tea."

The call disconnected. The weekend was just what Gabby needed to reset after what happened on her birthday and what Jules labeled as "Joe-Gate." Maybe she would check some of her matches when she got home. It felt good to get out and just let loose. There were no strings attached to Jake, but being around him felt right. It made her wonder if there was something still there. But it also boosted her confidence to continue to date and put herself out there a bit.

Gabby opened the door to her place and was, as usual, greeted by a disgruntled Bartleby. On the side table was a note that read *"A wise woman can predict the future because she creates it."* It was Jules' handwriting, of course. And that is one of the million reasons she was such a great friend. She lifted you up. Straightened your crown.

Gabby sat down at the end of her chaise and opened one of the boxes she brought back with her. At the top was Mark Woofalo. She picked him up and immediately could smell Jake's cologne on the stuffed dog. *Gahhh! I love how he smells.* Mr. Woofalo would be sitting on her bed from now on, and she hoped it retained Jake's scent for as long as possible. Her phone chimed, notifying her she had a text. Coincidentally, it was from none other than Jake.

Hey, it was really good to see you. I hope I can see you again soon.

It was good to see him, Gabby thought with a smile. She had to remind herself that she did not want to jump into a relationship with anyone anytime soon, despite how safe and familiar it felt with Jake. She didn't want to fool herself. And a lot of time had passed since she dated Jake seriously. Gabby was a different person. But they had the foundation of a good friendship, and she hoped that would never change.

Gabby text back: *Me too. Let's meet for lunch soon!*

She started scrolling through the Match-Up app. *Nope. Nope. Hmmm … he's kind of cute. Blonde. I don't usually go for blondes. But he has a bad boy "Charlie Hunnam" kind of look to him. Maybe …*

Then she saw it. The envelope with the "1" in the corner. Gabby opened her message inbox, and there was a message from Joe Gallant. She deleted the message without even reading it. *I have no desire whatsoever to read whatever that asshat has to say.*

"Well Mr. B., time to get ready for bed. I have to double check my sales quota and check on my clients first thing in the a.m."

Bartleby cocked his head to the side and gave a little meow of understanding, then weaved himself in and out and around Gabby's legs as she washed her face.

Gabby plugged in her phone and scrolled through photos from the weekend. She stopped at a picture of Jake with his arm around her neck. He was smiling, and Gabby had her head thrown back in a laugh. She loved his smile. Gabby missed that life sometimes. It was so much simpler then. No real responsibilities other than my job at Long Grove.

Shit!! I forgot Jule's Myrtles!! Ugh, I will never hear the end of it tomorrow.

With that, Gabby set her phone on her nightstand, put on her sleep mask, and drifted off to a pleasant story titled "Another Perfect Fall Day."

Chapter Eight

Gabby sat down at her desk and got settled in. She picked up her phone and was pleasantly surprised to have a Match-Up message from the blonde last night. His name was Josh. He wanted to meet her at Ed Debevic's followed by a movie. Ed Debevic's was a kitschy restaurant where the waiters were rude and stopped to dance along the countertops. It was a bit quirky, but he was cute and why not? They made plans to meet after work.

Jules loudly cleared her throat. "Uhhhh … something of the chocolatey goodness nature is missing from my desk this morning."

"I know … I know. I am so sorry I forgot. I promise to make it up to you."

"I will forgive you only on account that your parents didn't tell you about the house and that you were busy with *Jakey* …"

Gabby was reading through her emails when she loudly said, "Fuuuuuckkkkk."

Jules popped up like a Jack-in-the-Box and immediately asked Gabby what was wrong.

"Urban Investments just cancelled their lower-level suite reservations! That motherfucker!!"

"Wait, wait, wait. The *same* Urban Investments that Joe worked at?"

"One and the same. They had about twenty-six games booked. That's half the season. Excuse me while I go vomit."

"Don't panic! There is always a big demand for lower levels to be booked and there is usually a wait list. I am sure we can find you a replacement booking."

"I just know this is his doing. Like, really? Screw me over every which way. Super awesome. He had sent me a message on the dating app, and I deleted it. I just noticed it last night. This is a huge cut into my sales quota. He must have a lot of pull over there."

"It will be okay. And you know guys like that will get theirs. Karma is a bitch!"

"Yeah, I know. I met her last week. She was blonde. No offense."

"None taken. Hey, why don't you show me that picture of Jake? Take a break. Get your mind off work for a minute. We can go for a walk around the concourse."

"If you don't mind Jules, another time. I'm spiraling and lacking some coping skills," Gabby said.

"Listen, I am here for you, friend. We will get through this. I'm sure Mack has a waiting list as well for those suites. Please don't panic," Jules said as she tried to comfort Gabby.

"I appreciate that. I'm going to…" Gabby pointed to her computer behind her and slowly spun around. Jules made a sympathetic face and returned to her own cubicle.

Another perk of working for the United Center was that there was an on-site gym employees could use. It wasn't a big secret that Gabby was not usually a fan of exercise, especially running. Her motto was "I only run if I am being chased."

But after the day Gabby had at work, she had to blow off steam. And thanks to Jules, she had a gym bag with workout clothes under her desk. She literally could not believe that Joe stooped so low as to pull out of their suite agreement. What else could she expect from a guy who lied to her for weeks and had a secret life she knew nothing about?

Gabby walked out of the locker room into the workout area. She had on her Asics running shoes, soft olive-green capri yoga pants, and a white tank top that read "Work out? I thought you said 'Takeout.'"

Gabby was straddling the treadmill while she programmed her settings to get ready for her walk/run when she noticed someone out of the corner of her eye climb onto the treadmill next to her.

"Hey, how's it going? Is it cool if I run next to you?"

Gabby didn't hear anyone speaking to her however, since her AirPods were in her ears. She liked to play her eclectic play list loudly when she exercised. It was the only thing that would push her through. She started running while old school gangsta rap played loudly in her ears.

Gabby saw a hand waving in her peripheral, so she glanced over. The guy who had winked at her in the cafeteria was on the treadmill next to her. *Oh God. What could this dude want?*

Gabby tucked a lock of hair that loosely fell out of her ponytail behind her ear, then pointed at her AirPods. She didn't want to be rude, so she pulled one out of her ear.

"Sorry?" Gabby said a bit breathlessly while she slowed to a walk. She was not coordinated enough to run and maintain a conversation.

"I was just wondering if you minded me running next to you."

Gabby said, "You're fine."

As she started to put her AirPod back in her ear, she realized he was still trying to talk to her.

"I've seen you around the building. Do you work here? My name is Lucas, but everyone calls me Fitz."

Gabby sighed internally and said, "Yes, I am an account executive for ticket sales of premium executive suites for the Blackhawks. Heard of them? The Hawks, I mean. Well, and the Bulls."

Fitz chuckled and said, "Yeah, I have heard of them. Both teams. That job title is a mouthful. I saw you in the cafeteria the other day. First time I've ran into you here in the gym, though."

"Yeah, I don't run much. Shitty day. I'm going to …" She waved her hand with the AirPod in it, so he knew she was pretty much done talking. "Nice to meet you."

She put her AirPod back in her ear and focused on channeling her anger and bad day into a productive run.

By the time Gabby was done with her walk/run intervals on the treadmill, she noticed her neighbor was gone.

He was definitely attractive, she thought. *But he didn't say where he worked in the building. And I never told him my name. Oh well.*

She took a quick shower and got ready for her date with the blonde, Josh.

Chapter Nine

Gabby stood outside of Ed Debevic's and looked around for her date to show up. She felt a tap on her shoulder and spun around. There stood Josh, and he looked nothing like his profile picture. Oh, he had blonde hair, but that is where the similarities ended. Josh wasn't *ugly*, but he was definitely no Charlie Hunnam, either. Josh's hair was parted to the side and looked a bit stiff with gel. He was short, even a tad shorter than Gabby. And his lips were way too thin for her liking. But she was not so shallow that she wouldn't get to know someone based on looks alone.

Gabby, being Gabby, was not going to bail on the date. *What could go wrong? I mean, what worse thing could possibly happen after what Joe put me through?*

"Gabby? Hello, I'm Josh," he said as he put out his hand to shake hers.

"Hi, I'm Gabby. And starving. Shall we go in?"

The hostess took them to their table, and after handing them menus said, "Eat and get out!"

Gabby laughed and pointed to the back of the hostess's shirt that read "Just be aware that good customer service will not be served here."

Josh said, "Fun fact: They just re-opened this place after the original location closed six years ago. Did you know that Ed Debevic is not even a real person?"

"I did know there used to be a location around my neighborhood," Gabby responded. "Did not know the other fun fact."

Their waitress appeared. "Hi, my name is Candy, and I will be your waitress tonight." She turned her attention to Josh and said, "You sure you don't need a kid menu?"

Gabby snorted.

"What can I start you off with?" Candy asked as she chewed and smacked her gum.

"Could I get a water?" Josh asked the waitress.

"Water. Shocking," Candy teased him. "What can I get you, Sugar?"

"Um, how 'bout a vanilla milkshake?"

"Good choice," Candy said. "Probably better than the choice you made by coming here with that guy."

Josh seemed to bristle a bit, which seemed odd to Gabby since he knew so many "fun facts" about the place. Surely, he knew that rudeness was their thing.

"Actually, I will take a vanilla milkshake too," Josh added.

Before Candy could antagonize him further, some of the waitstaff hopped onto the counter and started dancing a routine to a loud rendition of "YMCA."

After the performance, Gabby asked, "Have you been here before?"

"I have been here a few times. Fun fact: actors David Schwimmer, Lamorne Morris, and Mark Ruffalo have all worked at Ed Debevic's at one time."

Gabby blurted out, "I have a stuffed dog named 'Mark Woofalo!'" She laughed. "My old boyfriend won it for me …" Her voice trailed off as she noticed Josh had a weird look on his face.

Candy was back to break up the awkwardness. Or add to it. "Listen, time is money, and I got a stack of bills at home that aren't about to pay themselves. What are you having?"

Josh asked, "What are your specials?"

"Nothing about this food is special. Next!" Candy shot back.

"BBQ pork sandwich for me and a side of onion rings," Gabby said while giggling. She loved BBQ anything. It was one of her favorites.

Josh said, "I'll take Mom's Meatloaf Sandwich."

"That tracks," Candy said as she gathered the menus and took off before anything else could be added.

"So, Josh, where do you work?" Gabby asked.

"I work at the Apple Store on Michigan Avenue," Josh responded. "I am an Apple Specialist – Retail Customer Service and Sales."

"Oh okay... well, I work at the United Center," Gabby started to say when Josh interrupted, "Fun fact: Did you know that the Chicago Blackhawks were established in 1926 and have won six Stanely Cup titles?"

"Um, I'm not sure if I knew those specific facts —"

Josh interrupted again to say, "Fun fact: Did you know that the United Center has been used as a filming location for several movies including *the Dark Knight* and *Transformers: Dark of the Moon*?"

OMG, this guy is effing rain main, Gabby thought sheepishly.

Gabby was grateful when their food arrived, and the conversation lulled. She felt a little less grateful when she realized Josh liked to speak with a mouthful of food. It was a major pet peeve of hers and grossed her out. The more he spoke, the more she realized that he was definitely not her type. He also sucked his teeth while he talked and seemed a bit too sensitive to suggest a place like Ed Debevic's for a first date.

The plan was to go to the movies after dinner, so Josh and Gabby drove separately to the AMC Theatre near the restaurant. *Why am I putting myself through this?* Gabby thought. *Because you are not a pretentious snobby bitch, Gabby!*

Josh bought tickets for the new *Ghostbusters* movie. As they walked into the theater, she followed Josh into a row, and he sat down right in front of another couple. It struck Gabby as odd. The theater was not crowded, why sit right in front of this other couple?

About halfway through the movie, the lady behind them received a call. Her phone rang loudly.

Kind of rude, Gabby thought. *Who doesn't put their phone on vibrate during a movie?*

Next thing she knew, the lady tapped Josh on the shoulder and said, "Your sister called. You left your cell phone at Ed Devebic's."

Josh didn't say anything and turned back in his seat.

What the ... who are these people? Should I sneak out? Go to the bathroom? Go for snacks? This is so awkward. Who needs their parents to chaperone a blind date at the movies? Especially at this age? Was his sister their waitress? I have so many questions.

She leaned over and whispered to Josh that she needed to use the restroom. *At my apartment.*

Gabby quickly walked to her Equinox and made her way home to River North. She felt incredibly guilty and knew that karma would be adding this to her list. But Josh would be okay. He had his mom and dad with him after all.

Gabby laughed out loud in her car. Jules would love this one.

Chapter Ten

As expected, Jules got a good laugh out of Gabby's horrible blind date. She was also very interested to hear about Gabby's encounter with Fitz at the company gym.

"Aren't you so glad I talked you into leaving gym clothes at work?" Jules asked. "Who knows, maybe you will "run" into this guy again? Shoot, maybe I will join you. Guess that's an opportunity to meet men I'm missing out on. But also, who were the mystery people at the movies? Did they look like Josh? Do you think they were his parents?"

"First off, I don't think the United Center is going to offer a free dating service perk anytime soon. And secondly, it was a dark theater, so I didn't get a good look. I have to assume they were his parents because the "mom" referenced his sister. Honestly, I didn't see a family resemblance between Josh and the waitress, Candy. But I wasn't looking for one, either. I think I could tweet this one to Jimmy Kimmel and have it make the cut for his bad dates segment."

Jules said, "I am so glad to be able to live vicariously through you. My life is not nearly as exciting."

"You sit on a throne of lies!! You just had a wild night out at Violet Hour!"

"Oh yeah! I can't believe I forgot to tell you. Evidently, I gave one of those guys my phone number. He came over last night."

"Well, glad you're here to tell the tale," Gabby laughed.

At the end of the day, Gabby shut down her computer and gathered her things to go home as she heard Jules say something from her cube.

"Yo! It's quittin' time, and the Hawks are hitting the ice in thirty. You in?"

"I don't know. My couch and a glass of red is calling my name," Gabby answered.

"We haven't hung out outside of work in forever. Hockey, hot guys, beer … much better than your couch and wine. You know it will be fun. You need this. I need this."

"Alright, alright," Gabby said. "Twist my arm. I'm in."

Gabby and Jules made their way to the employee elevator to head up to the corporate suite.

"Okay, so fill me in on this non-murderer you met," Gabby joked with Jules.

"His name is Trevor, and he is a day trader by day and a DJ by night.
And OMG, the sex last night was muy caliente! I'm so glad he called."

"I'm so glad you didn't end up on *Dateline*," Gabby teased.

"I made sure he was properly vetted before I spent any time alone with him!" Jules joked back.

Once they got to the suite, Gabby grabbed some bottled water and a hot dog as she made her way out to the seats in the front. Jules sat down next to her with a big cup of beer. The announcer was reading off the starting lineups for both teams.

"Welcome Hawks fans to the United Center! Tonight is an Original Six matchup. The Chicago Blackhawks vs. the Detroit Red Wings."

When he got done announcing the Wings players, the announcer continued, "And now the starting lineup for your Chicago Blackhawks! At center, #17, Lucas Fitzgerald!"

The crowd erupted in cheers as Gabby started choking on her water.

"You okay?" Jules asked.

"That guy … Lucas … Fitz … whatever … he's the guy from the cafeteria the other day. And the gym the other night. I had no idea who he was. I assumed he worked in another boring department or something."

"He works in another department alright," Julies said. "And he's cute too! Look at him!"

Gabby stared at the scoreboard in the middle of the arena where Lucas' pic was shown along with his teammates. *Yep, that's him.*

"He is cute. I mean, all we did was have a short conversation. But I feel so bad for blowing him off. I feel like an idiot."

"Aw, don't be so hard on yourself," Jules tried to comfort her. "That was a really rough day. So bad you actually made it to the gym," Jules joked.

"Haha. You're right. Dating life has been so rough lately. Work has been rough. Just having a pity party tonight."

"You know what helps with that? Beer!" Jules yelled as she jumped up to cheer as the Blackhawks scored a goal.

After the game, Gabby and Jules were walking to their cars as they heard, "Hey! Ticket Sales!"

The girls turned around and there was Fitz, showered and dressed in Blackhawks warmups as he walked toward them.

Jules elbowed Gabby. "Text me when you get home!"

Gabby watched as Jules walked away and then turned toward Fitz when he reached her. "Oh …

hey ... so ... I guess you *have* heard of the Chicago Blackhawks."

"Yeah, I have," Fitz laughed. "Did you catch the game? Do you watch a lot of them?"

"Yeah, Jules," she pointed toward Jules' car pulling out of the parking lot, "that's Jules. She's my best friend and co-worker. We sometimes go to home games after work. I'm Gabby, by the way. I don't think I told you my name last night."

"No, you didn't. Sorry I interrupted your run."

"Oh, it's fine. You're fine. I just had a rough day."

"I'm sorry to hear that. Would like to hear more about it if you want to share. There's a bar around the corner that my teammates and I sometimes go to after games. Do you want to grab a drink with me?"

"Let me preface what I'm about to say. I have had a few really rough dates lately. I mean, super recently, so I am going to pass on tonight. Raincheck?"

"A few rough dates, huh?" Fitz asked.

"You have no idea. Let's just say one guy was married, and the other guy brought his parents along," Gabby laughed.

"Yikes. Well, a raincheck is definitely in order. I promise you that I am not married. Nor would I bring my mom along." Fitz smiled.

Gabby laughed and said, "Well, good. I'm glad we got that out of the way." She stopped at her car. "Well, this is me."

"Don't take this the wrong way, but are you living in our car? What is up with all the boxes?" Fitz asked.

Gabby looked confused at first and then looked at her car and laughed. "No, I'm not unhoused. Not that that's a laughing matter. I am very passionate about helping people! My parents are selling my childhood home, and I packed some stuff up last weekend. I have been a little lazy with getting everything out of my car and into my apartment."

"Could I get your phone number? You know… regarding the raincheck and all. Or to help you get all this stuff out of your car." Fitz smiled again.

He is so sweet. And handsome.

"Yeah, sure. Give me your phone and I'll put my number in," Gabby said.

Their fingers brushed as Fitz handed Gabby his cell. She was surprised how it affected her as she felt the heat rise to her cheeks. She hoped Fitz didn't notice as she typed in her number.

"Have a good night, Fitz. See you around," Gabby said as she climbed into her car.

"I hope so," Fitz said with a wink.

Gabby grabbed her phone off her nightstand to text Jules before bed.

G: *I'm home. Safe and sound.*

J: *Already?? What about that Fitz guy? What happened? What did he say to you?*

G: *Oh, he asked if I wanted to have a drink. I gently turned him down in light of recent events. I did say yes to a raincheck, however.*

J: *Jules approves. Glad you agreed. See you tomorrow.*

Just as Gabby placed her phone on the charger, it dinged with another text notification. Gabby groaned. *So tired. Need sleep, Jules.* But the message was not from Jules.

If you don't have plans for lunch tomorrow, do you want to meet me at the Billy Goat? the message read.

Gabby texted Jake back: *Can't turn down a cheezborger!*

Gabby got back a laughing-crying emoji and *Cheezborger, cheezborger! No Pepsi – Coke! No fries – chips!*

Gabby text back a laughing-crying emoji and *How about one-ish?*

See you then, Jake said.

Bartleby mewed his approval and curled up close to Gabby's side.

"It's not a date, Mr. B. It's Jake. And it's just lunch. With an old friend."

Chapter Eleven

The following morning flew by as Gabby stayed busy making sure the suite that "he who shall not be mentioned" screwed her over on was filled and booked.

"What are your lunch plans today?" Jules asked as she gathered her purse.

"I am actually having lunch with Jake. He texted me last night. He is going to swing by and pick me up."

Gabby was looking in her compact mirror to make sure she looked presentable. She would be lying if she said she didn't put in some extra effort into her hair and outfit that day. The sides of her hair were gathered up on the top of her head and pinned with bobby pins. She had on a white button-down long-sleeved shirt with navy stripes. Gabby had rolled up the sleeves just a bit and also had the first few buttons undone on the top. She wore straight navy slacks that tapered at the ankle, a carved brown leather belt, and navy heels.

"Little nooner, eh? A little afternoon delight?" Jules teased with a few eyebrow raises.

Gabby rolled her eyes and said, "It's *not* a date. It's Jake. And it's just lunch. I will see you in an hour."

"Who are you trying to convince?" Jules asked with a wink.

As Gabby stepped out of the United Center building, Jake rolled up in a black Cadillac STS. She bent over to talk through the rolled-down window.

"Look at you, Mr. Fancy Pants."

"You like? I just picked it up last night. Get in – I'm starving."

Gabby slid in, and immediately the scent of Jake's cologne hit her. She smiled as she remembered the last time they were together. How great he smelled. How much fun they had bowling and hanging out. The kisses …

"What do you think? Gabby?" Jake snapped and waved his hands in front of Gabby's face. "Where are you?"

She blushed and said, "Oh, just a lot on my mind. Work ... you know. Sorry! What were you saying?"

"I was telling you that my mom said there has been a lot of traffic at your parents' house. Lots of interest. I wanted to know if you still had stuff to pack and move. I asked how you felt about the house possibly selling soon," Jake said.

"Yeah, that's still a sore topic with me. I do have some boxes in my car. The rest of the stuff I think I will grab at Thanksgiving," Gabby said.

"Well, let me know how I can help," Jake said. "I will be around that weekend as well."

"I appreciate that. If you're not busy this weekend, maybe you can help me carry up the boxes in my car?"

"Anything for you." Jake reached over and squeezed her thigh as he pulled into a parking spot at the famous Billy Goat Tavern.

Gabby jumped a bit at his touch and hoped he didn't notice. She definitely had butterflies. *Yep, that will do it. Gah! Reel it in, Gabby.*

If you are from the Chicago area, you know about the tavern and the curse of the billy goat. It was a spot made of legends and had a rich history. The place still had wood-paneled walls and a floor that had seen better days. But as iconic as the food was, Gabby thought it had the best atmosphere for people-watching.

After they sat down with their food, Jake told her about his big promotion that led him to buy his first new car as an adult. Gabby was listening, but her mind wandered as she stared at Jake while he talked. She tried to think of a time when she saw Jake dressed like he was. Prom? *No, not that fancy.* High school football banquet? Graduation? He was very handsome in his black slacks, white button-down oxford shirt, and black suit jacket. No tie today. And glasses! He wasn't wearing his contacts. *How could one person make glasses look that sexy?* Gabby thought.

"Look at us with our grown-up jobs. Who knew?" Gabby joked.

Suddenly, Jake stopped mid-sentence to say, "Oh my god. Did you see who just walked in?"

Gabby looked up to see three guys walk through the door and get in line to order.

"That's Alex DeBrincat, Lucas Fitzgerald, and Adam Gaudette!" Jake said, a little too excitedly.

He then started talking about hockey stats, the Blackhawks, and much more, but Gabby zoned out. She knew Jake was a sports nut and loved the Blackhawks. She loved sports too, but the stats bored her.

Gabby slowly ate her chips one by one, chewing thoughtfully while dropping a few "mmhmms" so Jake didn't feel ignored. She glanced Fitz's way every now and then to check him out while he was standing in line. She could appreciate that he was a good-looking guy. Through their limited conversations, he also seemed like a very nice guy.

Jake stopped talking and stared at Gabby over her shoulder. The three hockey players walked toward their table, but her back was to them. After they passed by, she couldn't help herself, and her eyes landed on Fitz's butt. Fitz turned around at the exact moment and smiled a big smile and gave Gabby a wink.

With a small wave, Fitz said, "Hey, Gabby."

Jake had to practically pick his jaw off the table. After the hockey players walked out of earshot, he said, "You know Lucas Fitzgerald? And you didn't tell me? We keeping secrets now?" he joked.

"I literally just met him. I don't really know him at all," Gabby defended.

"Maybe you could get me his autograph. If that's not too much to ask. Is that weird? That's weird. Don't ask him."

"Honestly, Jake, if I knew him well enough, I would ask him for you. Should I ask *him* for a ride back to the United Center? You know, so I can get to know him better and get an autograph for you?" Gabby teased.

"Nah, I got dibs on you first."

The flirting made Gabby smile and her heart

skip a beat. "Oh, you think so, huh?"

This is NOT a date, Gabby reminded herself.

Not. A. Date.

Chapter Twelve

The weeks during the beginning of the season were so hectic that Gabby didn't know if she was coming or going. At work, she was busy making sure her clients were happy and having their needs met. *But who is meeting your needs, Gabby?* she thought to herself. She needed an outlet. Needed to cut loose after work and blow off some steam in more ways than one.

She and Fitz were texting back and forth a bit, trying to coordinate their schedules to meet for that drink. His game and practice schedule were more complicated than hers of course, and their text conversations were mainly the exchange of pleasantries. Gabby started to wonder if they had much in common or if he was worth the trouble.

Jake had also been busy, along with Jules. Her friends back home didn't live close enough to hang out on the drop of a dime. Gabby was craving some companionship. So, she decided to go on a few dates with some guys she was matched with on the Match-Up app. They were all technically supposed to be "one-offs." If she connected with someone, great. Gabby was not so invested that she was worried about getting hurt.

In true Gabby fashion, the dates were so bad that they were one and done. Jules made time every morning to revel in the sordid details. So much so that she actually popped popcorn one morning and started to give Gabby "challenges." That week it was five first dates in five days. Which went something like this:

Date #1: They went to dinner at some obscure restaurant. He (whose name was also random and not worth noting) barely spoke throughout the entire night. After they both did the bill tango, Gabby's date paid the bill, and she left the tip. Gabby excused herself to the restroom, and on her way back, she saw her date pocket the tip money.

Date #2: The next date we will call "Rob." Gabby and Rob met at a popular chain restaurant. While they ate, Rob told Gabby that his ex was a waitress at that very restaurant. He said he loved to bring dates there to piss her off. Gabby suddenly wondered if she should be worried that his ex spit in her food.

Date #3: This date was with a guy we will call "Chris." Chris's family owned a local diner. Chris joked that he told his entire family about Gabby and wanted her to meet them. They were all at the diner the night of their first date. Think: *"My Big Fat Greek Wedding"* meets "awkward first and last date."

Date: #4: Gabby met "James" at the Violet Hour for drinks after work. She thought things were going pretty well. Well enough that she felt comfortable inviting James up for a nightcap. Gabby and James were in the middle of a pretty heated make out sesh when James broke down crying. He told Gabby he thought he might be gay.

Date #5: While it seemed entirely impossible to top any of the dates that week, here comes "Don." Gabby also met Don for drinks. Don spent the entire time talking about how men were superior to women. He even quoted several "scientific studies" to support his pig-headed, misogynistic attitude.

By Friday, Gabby was exhausted, and Jules was thoroughly amused and entertained. They had plans to go to the Blackhawk's game, but all Gabby could think about was curling up with Bartleby and a good book.

When she got home from work, she kicked off her shoes and sat down on the couch. She scrolled through her phone to muster up the energy to order takeout delivery. Indecisiveness got the best of her, so she paused her search to send Jake a text.

G: *Hey you. I know you have been super busy lately, but do you have time for me tomorrow?*

Jake immediately text back: *I* always *have time for you. What's up?*

G: *I wondered if you wouldn't mind me getting the last of the stuff from my car. I will pay you in tacos.*

J: *Will work for tacos. But would also do it for free. What time do you want me?*

Oh, so many things I could say to answer that question, Gabby thought.

G: *Does 5:00 p.m. work for you? Shouldn't take us more than an hour and will give us plenty of time to work up an appetite.*

J: *I could think of a few things we could do to work up an appetite that would be way more fun…*

G: *Keep it in your pants, Rogers. Seriously, though. Thank you. I appreciate it.*

The next day, Jake was right on time and worked diligently to help Gabby unload the last of the boxes from her car. Using the trolley her dad lent her and having an elevator in the building helped. And having Jake to help her really lessened the burden of it all. Of course, he looked adorable with his backward baseball hat. He still had that boyish charm.

"I can't believe I had never seen your place before today!" Jake exclaimed. "You need to give me a tour."

"I can't believe you were living in the city and didn't bother to tell me," Gabby admonished.

"Touché," Jake added. "Do you remember when I helped move you into your dorm freshman year of college?"

"I do remember. I also remember you bitching about how much stuff I had accumulated and felt that I HAD to bring along to school with me," Gabby laughed. "It's probably all the same stuff you just moved out of my car."

"I guess we have come full circle," Jake said as he moved toward Gabby.

He gently grabbed her arm and pulled her in closer to him. She wrapped her arms around his waist and sighed. After a few moments, Gabby heard Jake's stomach rumble.

"I do appreciate you helping me today," Gabby chuckled. "Also, your stomach is growling really loud."

She laughed and pulled away. "I will call in our order. Tacos were promised!"

They ate takeout from Seoul Taco and watched a couple of Netflix movies. Jake grabbed one of her giant Northwestern blankets and held it up.

"Girl, I am going to have to get you a Michigan blanket to replace this one," he teased.

They snuggled under the purple and white blanket anyway. It felt really good to be that close to Jake and have his arms around her. Even Bartleby didn't mind having him around. It was nice to spend time together with no other expectations, even though Gabby was having a hard time not thinking about the "what ifs."

When it was time to call it a night, Gabby walked Jake to the door. He turned and bent down to kiss her. Those full, familiar lips would never get old. Damn, he was a good kisser. Jake pressed himself against Gabby enough to make her consider asking him to stay.

"Thanks for the company tonight. It was just what I needed. I do love spending time with you, Jake."

"I wouldn't mind doing this more often," Jake murmured.

After one more lingering kiss, Gabby ushered Jake out. She closed the door and leaned against it, her heart racing as Bartleby circled around her legs. She scooped him up and nuzzled his neck as she walked over to her bookshelf.

Gabby picked up a copy of a new romance novel that Addy recommended, *Heart Bones* by Colleen Hoover. It was about a girl and a guy who come from two very different worlds. *Like a football player and journalist. Or maybe even a hockey player and an account executive.*

She giggled as she crawled into bed with
Bartleby and her book, and she read until she fell
asleep with her book open where she left off next to
her.

Chapter Thirteen

It was "Giving Tuesday." Gabby and her co-workers were volunteering at the Greater Chicago Food Depository. She and Jules were at a table organizing and boxing up food donations for the residents of Chicago. Gabby had on a pair of leggings, a long-ish sweatshirt that read "Hockey is my favorite season," and a pair of shell toed Addidas tennis shoes. Mack told the staff to dress comfortably, be ready to work, and possibly get dirty.

Gabby's parents had taken Gabby to many events throughout the years to show her the importance of giving back to the community. They served at shelters and food banks. They delivered Christmas presents to foster families. They collected non-perishables and healthcare items for the unhoused. Giving back and serving the community was in Gabby's blood.

The Food Bank Director spoke to the group. "Hello everyone! Thank you for being here. One in five Chicago households are experiencing food insecurities. We appreciate your willingness to serve your community and take time out of your busy day. We also have a special announcement. We are so happy, fortunate, and proud to say that your very own Chicago Blackhawks will be joining us today!"

Gabby and Jules immediately looked at each other. Gabby was wide-eyed, and Jules laughed loudly. Almost simultaneously, Gabby felt a tall presence next to her as a very nice smelling cologne filled the air around her. *Is that Burberry?*

"Hey, Ticket Sales!" Fitz said.

Why does he have to smell so good? And look so good?

Gabby tried to control her face and voice as she replied, "I do have a name ya know. Remember

… Gabby? Too many checks from behind got your brain scrambled?"

"Funny *and* knows her hockey!" Fitz said. "Finally, we are in the same place at the same time. I was hoping you were going to be here today."

"Here I am!" Gabby awkwardly laughed. "I'm surprised you recognized me with this super sexy plastic hair bonnet on."

"You make it look good," Fitz said as he put on his own bonnet, plastic apron, and disposable gloves.

Just then the Food Bank Director split them into groups. "The food we receive comes in bulk qualities. We need you to break it down to manageable sizes." As he pointed Jules and Gabby's way, he said, "This group over here will repack bulk dry goods such as pasta, rice, and beans into smaller quantities. This group over here will be sorting produce, inspecting, and boxing shipments of bread.

Lastly, the group over there will be asked to load the Sprinter vans so we can properly and efficiently distribute this quality food to participating food pantries, soup kitchens, and shelters that we partner with. Once again, thank you for your service."

"Welp, looks like I have the van loading job," Fitz said.

Gabby smiled and gave him a little wave as she and Jules started to walk to their assigned station.

Suddenly, Fitz called out, "Hey, Gabby, do you want to grab lunch after this? Cash in on that raincheck?"

A sharp elbow to the side made Gabby glare at Jules before responding, "Sure. Billy Goat Tavern? I will meet you over there when we are done here."

Gabby and Jules spent the morning boxing up items and putting the boxes on shelves near a loading dock, then others loaded them into vans to disperse to the community. Every time Gabby glanced up, she would notice Fitz looking at her. It made her smile and blush a little. A few times when she was bringing a box over, Fitz would go over and take it from her, so she didn't have to carry it. *So chivalrous.*

A few hours later, Gabby sat at the bar at the tavern. She didn't have to wait long before Fitz walked in. As she watched him walk all the way over to where she sat, she thought, *He's a good-looking guy. Tall. Maybe 6'2", athletic build, thick chestnut hair ... Fitz was definitely easy on the eyes. He could give Jake a run for his money. Not that there is any sort of competition going on.*

"I'll have what she's having. Vodka tonic?"

Gabby said, "Water. I am going back to the office after lunch. Not really into day-drinking when I work." *Stop being a smart ass, Gabriella! Damn. I'm channeling my mom.*

"Fair enough. Sorry, that was dumb of me," Fitz said as he sat down beside her. "Nice sweatshirt, by the way. So, I know where you work and what you do for the most part. I want to know more about you, Gabby."

Why does the way he says my name sound so sexy?

"Well, I grew up in Buffalo Grove. My parents were high school teachers. I have lived in Chicago since I graduated college. How long have you played for the Blackhawks? Sorry, I don't have your trading card."

Fitz laughed. "I have been playing with the Blackhawks since I entered the draft four years ago. I've pretty much played hockey my entire life. I didn't really peak until my late teens and wasn't drafted until I was twenty."

"Starting line-up. You must be decent." Gabby took a drink of her water.

"Oh, so you *were* watching me." Fitz looked impressed. "I do okay. But I've worked really hard to get to where I am today. I take nothing for granted."

"I wasn't *not* watching." Gabby smiled. "But you could have told me who you were at the gym."

"I could have," Fitz said, "but I would like you to know who I am outside of the game of hockey."

"Fair enough," Gabby said. "I have a little confession to make. I have heard your name before but didn't put two and two together. Now I feel like the silly one."

"Can I get you two anything to eat?" the bartender asked as he handed Fitz and Gabby menus.

Fitz looked at the menu and asked Gabby, "Want to get a couple of appetizers to share?"

"Sure, sounds great."

"Do you have any siblings?" Fitz asked after he ordered some nachos and pretzel bites.

"Nope, just me. But I was not a spoiled only child," Gabby clarified. "My parents expected me to work hard for the things I wanted. You?"

"I was raised by a single mom. One older brother and one younger brother. My mom sacrificed a lot for my brothers and me."

Gabby was impressed. "That's really admirable."

The bartender sat the appetizers in front of them and walked away as Fitz and Gabby reached for a pretzel bite at the same time. Once again, she felt the heat rise to her cheeks as Fitz's fingers brushed hers.

"Ladies first." Fitz gestured toward the plate.

Their conversation moved to their feelings on volunteering. It was important to Fitz because he was motivated by the memory of hunger. He could relate all too well to the people they were serving.

"I want to make sure I stay humble," he said. "Never forget where I came from."

Gabby nodded. "I honestly feel like our whole purpose in life… why we were placed on this earth, is to serve one another. To take care of one another."

Fitz stared at Gabby for a moment. She hadn't really noticed his eyes before. They were amber-colored and sparkled in a way. He smiled with his eyes.

"You are incredible," he complimented.

"Oh, I don't know about all that." Gabby blushed and looked down at her lap.

Fitz asked, "I hope this isn't too forward, but do you have a boyfriend? You were having lunch here the other day with a guy. Sorry if that's nosy. I would like to see you again, but I didn't want to assume either."

"Oh, he's just an old friend from high school," Gabby explained. *Right?* Her internal monologue tried to keep her in check.

When they finished eating, Fitz walked Gabby out to her car. He bent down and peeked in the windows. "Hey! You're no longer living out of here."

Gabby laughed and said, "Yeah, my friend helped me unload everything. Thank you for the company and conversation. I'm sure I will be seeing you soon. Seems like that happens a lot these days."

"I really hope so." Fitz grinned. "Hey, I have some early practices coming up. Would you be up to hanging out after you are done working for the day?"

"Yeah, that sounds great," Gabby said as she

climbed in her car. "Text me?"

"Count on it." Fitz grinned.

Chapter Fourteen

It was Thanksgiving. The last one Gabby would celebrate in her childhood home. She was in the kitchen, cooking with her mom and feeling a bit melancholy.

"How is work going, honey? You don't seem like yourself," Gabby's mom asked her.

"Oh, you know. It's a bit stressful. I lost a big account but was able to recoup the losses. And just being here, knowing this is the last time we will bake in this kitchen, makes me extremely sad."

Gabby's mom reached up and grabbed a small box from the top shelf of the pantry. It was pushed all the way to the back, and Gabby had never seen it before.

"What's this?" Gabby asked.

"That's where Grandma kept the good stuff," her mom said.

"The good stuff?" Gabby was confused. She opened the box to find several handwritten recipes in her grandmother's handwriting: from scratch meatballs, sausage stuffing, potato soup, homemade bread, biscuits, stone jar cookies, and more.

"Gabby, food ties people and families together. This kitchen is the heart of our home, correct? It's where we have made the best memories. But we can also find those memories living on through these recipes and food traditions. What do you notice about those cards?"

"They are all written in Gram's handwriting."

"Yes, flip one over."

Gabby flipped over several recipe cards to find other handwritten notes. Some were grocery lists. Some were messages about where a recipe came from. Some said simply "I love you, you know" and one read "All in due time."

Gabby looked at her mom with tears in her eyes. "Those are yours to keep," her mom said. "The smell and tastes of those special recipes will always help you recall the fond memories of family and the time we all spent together."

Gabby hugged her mom, then the two of them gathered up the side dishes and placed them on the dining table where Gabby's dad was standing in front of the turkey. He was so proud standing there with a carving knife in one hand and a smile on his face. It made Gabby feel so proud. Her parents had given her such a wonderful life.

Gabby sat down next to her Gram and kissed her cheek. It would also likely be the last Thanksgiving her Gram would be present. She looked around the table at her grandmother, her aunt and uncle, and two cousins who were sitting at the table. Her heart swelled. She loved the holidays and the family time. It was bittersweet to think this would be the last Thanksgiving they could all be together in that house.

Her mom said, "Who would like to say grace?"

"Grace? She died thirty years ago!!"

"Honestly, Gabby," her mom said with an eye roll. Gabby's two teenage cousins laughed at the Christmas movie reference.

Gabby's dad led a beautiful Thanksgiving prayer, carved the turkey, and then the room was filled with clinking silverware and dishes. Laughter and chatter. Veronica Price always did a beautiful job decorating for the holidays. She put out her finest china that her father brought back from Japan during the war. There were candles lit in the middle of the table surrounded by fall decorations. The sideboard along the wall held a pumpkin pie made from scratch, along with an apple pie and a pecan pie.

Gabby was not one to worry about indulging during the holidays. Besides, if her pants were feeling tight, she could always hit the gym as a last resort after work. Her mind drifted to thinking about Fitz, and she smiled. They had been texting back and forth getting to know one another. He really seemed genuinely interested in learning about her more and more. He asked all kinds of questions about her likes and dislikes, hobbies, and how she liked to spend her spare time. Gabby wondered when she would see him next because the more she got to know him, the more she wanted to have that official first date.

Just then, Gabby's phone vibrated.

Happy Turkey Day! It was a text from Fitz. It made her heart flutter. He was thinking of her. She was thinking of him. Gabby smiled.

Happy Turkey Day to you too!

Gabby happened to look out the dining room window that faced Jake's house. She saw Jake throwing a football around in the yard with his two brothers and some of his cousins. She couldn't help but feel that he would always have a piece of her heart. She knew Jake wouldn't mind more of a relationship with Gabby. And honestly, Gabby wouldn't mind it, either. But their last break up was very hard on her. She didn't want her heart to get broken again. And after the group chat with the female side of the Infinity Squad, she gathered no one was really a fan of that option.

After washing the last of the dishes, Gabby told her mom she was going to grab her coat and walk next door to see if Jake was still there. Gabby knocked on the door, and Jake's mom opened it.

"Oh, Gabby! How are you?" She welcomed her with a big hug. "Jake! Gabby's here," his mom yelled behind her.

Jake came up from their finished basement. He had on a pair of sweats and an old high school football sweatshirt. They could have been seventeen again, standing in the foyer. His hair was all tousled like he just woke up from a nap. He was dressed so casual and cute.

"Nice to see you again, Gabby," Jake's mom said.

"Thanks, Maryann. It is always nice to see you as well. Hey, can we talk?" Gabby asked Jake.

"Sure, let me grab my coat," Jake replied.

They walked over to the brick patio behind Gabby's house, and Jake knelt and lit a fire. He sat down next to Gabby on the bench and snuggled near her. Gabby welcomed the snuggle and put her head on his shoulder, and Jake moved his arm around her to move her closer to his body.

After a few moments of silence, Gabby asked, "What is going on with us, Jake?"

"What do you mean?"

"I mean, whenever we are around each other, we fall back into old patterns. The other night when you were over, it felt like, I don't know. Like we were *together-together.* It's confusing. I have been trying hard to focus on me and not be serious about anyone. But things are different with you. Like the rules don't apply."

"I don't mean to cause you extra grief," Jake said. "I love being around you. I love hanging out with you. We don't have to label anything."

Jake leaned in close to Gabby. *How could he smell and look this good when he also looks like he just rolled out of bed?*

Gabby closed her eyes as Jake leaned over and put his full, soft lips on hers.

Chapter Fifteen

Jules was at Gabby's place the following Saturday. They hung out, drank wine, and talked while getting ready to go out.

Gabby turned side to side in her bedroom in front of her full-length gold mirror. She had on a short sleeve white blouse shirt with a deep "v" that tucked into ripped skinny jeans that were a light wash. She also wore her cute tan heels that strapped around her ankle. Her hair was piled into a messy bun on top of her head.

"You look hot, girl!" Jules said when Gabby walked into the living room.

"You know, I feel good. I am excited to go out!"

Jules had a glass of Riesling in one hand and was running her fingertips along Gabby's bookshelves and reading titles aloud.

"Fitzgerald, Hemingway, Morrison, Angelou ... *Twilight* and *Fifty Shades of Gray*?" She turned around and raised an eyebrow at Gabby.

"Don't you book shame me! I have a very eclectic collection. I also have everything Stephen King has ever written. My TBR pile is tall, and I still find myself checking books out from the library every now and then."

"Speaking of Fitzgerald ... Fitz. What's going on with him? Have you heard from him?"

"We have been texting back and forth. Getting to know each other. And then there's Jake. I can't get either one of them out of my head. It's kind of messing with me."

"You know what you need?" Jules asked.

"I can only imagine where this is going."

"A palette cleanse! You need a night out to get your mind off these two guys. Let's go have a good time and see what – or who – the night brings!"

Gabby and Jules arrived at the Sound Bar around 11:00 p.m. The place was packed. The lights flashed and the bass thumped. Trevor, the guy who Jules was having "hot sex with," was DJing.

"Let's go get drinks!" Jules shouted at Gabby.

Gabby and Jules walked to the nearest bar and ordered a couple of drinks – two rum and cokes.

"I'm going to go say hi to Trevor. Do you want to come with?"

Gabby shook her head and leaned up against the wall. She was a people watcher. She moved to the music as she stood in one place and scanned the room. Gabby moved off the wall to see where Jules went when she spotted him.

Fitz stood across from Gabby and stared at her. His gaze was intense, and it felt like he had been staring at her for some time. He had on a tight-fitting black V-neck shirt and jeans. And he looked hot as hell.

Gabby's heart felt like it was thumping as loud as the bass, and she stood there, never breaking eye contact as Fitz walked over. When he got to her, he took her empty plastic cup, set both his drink and her empty one on the bar and pulled her onto the dance floor.

She didn't recognize the music but couldn't help moving her body. The vibe was indiscernible. Fitz held her close and danced behind her. They moved together fluidly. Every now and then, Fitz would bend down and kiss her neck, which sent chills down to Gabby's toes. When he did that, she would find herself reaching back and running her hands through the back of his hair. She closed her eyes; they could have been the only ones in the club.

Fitz turned Gabby around and put his hands around her waist and pulled her as close to him as he could.

OMG … I can feel his … OMG. Her mind raced.

He bent down and kissed Gabby, and she kissed him back. Had they not been in a crowded club, she had no idea how far it could have gone.

"Hey, I will be right back," Fitz said into Gabby's ear. The hot air sent shivers down her spine. "Will you wait for me?"

Gabby could do nothing other than nod her head. As Fitz walked away, she walked over to where she had been standing as she caught her breath.

She thought Fitz was back when she felt someone standing next to her – until she heard his voice.

"Who the fuck was that?"

Startled, Gabby turned to see Joe Gallant standing there. "You have to be kidding. You have no right," she said angrily. "In fact, you have some *balls* to be even standing here trying to speak to me!"

Joe grabbed Gabby's arm and said, "Maybe we should step outside so we can speak privately."

"I have nothing to say to you. Whatever we had is over. Zero regrets!" Gabby shouted as she tried to shake him loose.

"I can see you are wearing the ring I bought you. It's not over for us, Gabby."

"You want the ring back? You can have the ring back!" Gabby yelled as she struggled to pull it off her finger. *Damn water retention!*

"Hey, you heard her. Back off bro," Fitz said, appearing out of nowhere.

"Who the fuck are you, tough guy?" Joe pushed Fitz in the chest.

"Joe stop! Just get the fuck out of here!" She turned her focus to Fitz. "He's not worth it. Please, trust me. Let's just go."

Fitz put his arm around Gabby and led her away while Joe continued to yell, "Walk away, you pussy! She's a little bitch anyway."

Fitz abruptly turned back and punched Joe Gallant square in the nose. Joe stumbled back as Gabby pulled on Fitz's arm and pled with him, "I just want to go. We need to find Jules."

Gabby pulled her phone out of her back pocket to text Jules: *Exit 911.*

Immediately, Jules text back: *Be right there.*

Once outside, Fitz was pacing as Gabby leaned against the brick building. Jules came out the door soon after.

"What the hell is going on? Is everything okay?"

"I need to get out of here. I need to go home," Gabby said.

Fitz turned to Jules. "I will get her home." He looked at Gabby and asked, "Is that okay with you?"

Gabby nodded. "Go back and hang with Trevor," she told Jules. "You still have your key to my place, right?"

Jules nodded and hugged Gabby tightly. "Are you sure about this?" she whispered in Gabby's ear.

"Yeah … I will fill you in when you get back," Gabby said.

"Well, this is me," Gabby said as she reached her apartment.

Fitz sighed and leaned against the wall next to her front door. "Are you going to be okay? I hate leaving you like this."

"To be honest, I would love to invite you in. But something tells me that maybe tonight was too emotionally charged for that to be a good idea," Gabby said as she ran her hand down Fitz's chest.

Fitz grabbed Gabby's waist and pulled her over to him as he leaned with his back against the wall. He cupped her face in his hands and kissed her deeply and passionately.

He smells so good. He tastes so good. He feels so good, Gabby thought.

Gabby pulled herself back to catch her breath a bit and said, "Um, I should get in there. I'm sure we are giving my nosy neighbor, Mrs. Miller a good show."

Fitz called over his shoulder and a bit too loudly said, "You're welcome!"

Gabby laughed. "Seeing you tonight was a pleasant surprise. Thank you for defending my honor. I'm sure I owe you an explanation but if it can wait for another time…"

"You owe me nothing," Fitz said as he tucked a loose lock of hair behind her ear that came down from her messy bun. "Will you text me tomorrow?"

"You can count on it," Gabby said with a wink and a quick and sweet kiss as she let herself into her apartment. She leaned against the door and gave her head a quick shake as if to erase only the bad portions of the night. *Tonight was too much to process. Things will look better in the morning.*

With that, Gabby went to her bathroom to get ready for bed.

Chapter Sixteen

Gabby rolled over and pulled up her eye mask. She reached to the side and grabbed her phone to check the time. 11:00 a.m. She got up and shuffled out to her kitchen to put on some coffee and pour a big, tall glass of ice water. She was dehydrated and had a cluster headache behind her right eye.

Jules lay on the couch with her back to Gabby and had her face buried in the sofa pillows. All Gabby could hear were muffled moans and groans.

"What time is it?" Jules mumbled.

"It's 11:00 a.m."

"I feel like I have been hit by a Mack truck."

"I'm not feeling quite as badly as you. Just a slight headache."

"Well, you probably burned off all the alcohol dancing, you sexy minx!"

"Oh god. Hardly. I have no words. I feel like I dreamt last night."

Suddenly, Jules rolled over and whispered, "Oh my god, is he … is Fitz in there??"

Gabby threw a couch pillow at Jules. "No! Though, to be honest, when I woke up and rolled over to check the time, I half expected him to be in my bed. What a wild night."

"What the hell happened, anyway?" Jules asked Gabby. "You were asleep when I got back, so I just crashed on the couch."

Gabby groaned and put her head between her hands. "Fitz and I were dancing, and I think he had to go to the bathroom or something. I was waiting for him when Joe came up to me and started questioning me about to who Fitz was and why was I still wearing the ring he gave me. And then, of course, Fitz came back to defend my honor, and it turned physical. It took a bit to get Fitz to walk away, but I am glad he did. He has a career to think about. Joe is just a piece of shit who should crawl back under the rock he came out from."

"I feel so bad that I was not there for you. I shouldn't have left you to hang out with Trevor," Jules said sadly.

"It's all good! Please, don't apologize. Fitz got me home all safe and sound. And before you ask, nothing else happened with him. Just a kiss goodnight. He's kind of amazing," Gabby smiled, remembering the better moments of the night.

"See, some of the night was fun! But so much for your palette cleanse. Unless Fitz cleaned it for you," Jules laughed as swirled her finger and pointed it at Gabby's mouth.

"Hardy har. What am I going to do about Fitz and Jake?"

"Have them both."

"That's so something you would say. I just don't want anyone to get hurt. But I like them both. There is no denying it."

"Maybe you should go back to dating randos for a bit on your dating app?"

"Yeah, maybe that is a good idea for the time being. Keep Fitz and Jake at arm's length for now. You want some coffee?"

"You got any cinnamon rolls?"

"You think I'm running a B&B here?"

Gabby started off her week with a couple dates from Match-Up. She kept it as casual as possible and took the opportunity to explore more of the Chicago breakfast food scene.

She met one date at Bad Owl for breakfast, where Gabby got their version of a Harry Potter Butterbeer and a hazelnut chocolate beignet. Both were divine. She briefly thought about dusting off her writing skills and writing a food blog on the side.

Another place, the Stockyard Coffeehouse, Gabby liked so much that she returned with her new Stephen King book and sat on the banquette in one of the big windows with cozy pillows and had a Mexican mocha coffee. Gabby was enjoying exploring new places. That was the great thing about Chicago; no matter how long she lived there, there were so many places to discover.

One night after work, Gabby convinced Jules to meet her at the Understudy Coffee and Books for trivia night. It was a new coffee shop Gabby discovered while planning one of her morning dates/food experiences. The bookshop café always had something happening: readings, live music, and even cabaret nights, and it was quickly becoming a new favorite place to hang out and keep her distracted.

Jules brought along her roommates, Marissa and Kelly. You were supposed to play with a team of four, but Gabby was not entirely sure of their *Friends* trivia knowledge. Fortunately, they all appointed Gabby "team leader" and the keeper of the trivia pen and paper.

"Welcome to Trivia Night at the Understudy! I will be your host, Monica! Yes, that is my real name. Yes, I know. It's ironic since tonight's theme is *Friends*," she said in her best "Monica" voice. "There will be two rounds of four questions worth one point each. Then there will be two bonus questions. The first one is worth five points, and the second one is

worth ten points. Two-Two-Two-Five-Ten-Two …"
Everyone started laughing. "Good luck!"

Gabby laughed and stopped when the other
three didn't laugh at all. "If you know, you know. Omg,
you don't know, do you? Am I going to have to fly
solo?" she laughed again.

"I know *some* of the show, Gabby," Jules said
incredulously.

"My apologies," Gabby giggled.

Host Monica said, "Okay, gang. Question one:
Where did Rachel buy the apothecary table?"

"I know this," Gabby whispered and wrote
Pottery Barn on her list.

"Question two: How many sisters does Joey
have? It's okay if you can't remember. Sometimes
Joey can't remember, either."

"Jules – do you know this one?" Gabby asked.

Jules said, "I don't remember. I feel like a lot since he is Italian."

"I'm going to write down five," Gabby said as she looked at Jules' roommates.

Marissa answered, "Don't look at us. We are only here for the booze and people watching."

Super, Gabby thought.

Host Monica spoke up again. "Question three: Which one has a twin?"

Jules whispered, "Easy. Phoebe!"

"Question four: Who wears all of Chandler's clothes at one time in a scene?"

Jules whispered, "I know this one too! Joey!"

"Good job, sister friend," Gabby said encouragingly to Jules.

"Alright all you *Friends* nerds. That completes round one. Someone will be around to collect your slips," Monica said. "Order a drink during this intermission and don't forget to tip your waitstaff!"

Marissa and Kelly were telling a riveting tale about some guys they hooked up with after one of their shifts at some restaurant where they were working. Gabby wasn't really paying attention as she scrolled through her phone mindlessly. They were nice enough, just not her cup of tea.

Host Monica reappeared after about ten minutes. "You all ready for round two? Remember, 'You don't tell me what to do. I tell *you* what to do.' Thank you. Here all night," she said again in her best "Monica" voice. "Question one …"

"Wait – I thought we already had question one?" Kelly leaned over to Marissa.

"No, that was round one. This is round two, question one," Marissa responded.

"I am so confused," Kelly said.

"Girls, shut your faces!" Jules said, annoyed. "I can't hear the question!"

Host Monica asked, "What is Chandler's full name?"

"Gah, what is this? It's a girly name, right?" Gabby asked Jules. "I've got it! Chandler Muriel Bing. Boo ya!"

Gabby's team didn't win trivia night, but she did succeed in achieving her goal of keeping busy and keeping her mind off Fitz and Jake. It was a win in her book.

Chapter Seventeen

Gabby could not deny the connection she had with Fitz. But she was also having a hard time letting Jake go. Gabby was unsure she even wanted to. She tried to imagine what it would be like to be in a real relationship with Jake again. It scared her a little because she felt they were trapped in an old mindset and not "adult Gabby and Jake." What would that look like if they decided they didn't like each other anymore after all? She did not expect to fall for a guy so soon after Joe-Gate, let alone two great guys.

Gabby relayed all her feelings to Jules as they walked around Christkindlmarket after work one evening. She had mulled cider in one hand and a stuffed pretzel in the other. The market was magical with all the vendor tents lined up around the plaza with white lights everywhere.

Gabby loved to buy little trinkets for herself and gifts for her parents every year. Plus, there was all kinds of delicious German goodies throughout. There were pierogies with onions, bacon, and sour cream on top. There were German sausages and fried potatoes. There were artisanal cheeses and German bread. And after all that, strudels, pastries, chocolate-covered fruit, marzipan, gingerbread, German cookies and chocolates, and a partridge in a pear tree. Gabby was in foodie heaven. Autumn was her favorite, but Christmas in Chicago could rival Rockefeller Centre in her opinion.

"Honestly, Gabby, I don't envy your predicament. I know we joke about things a lot, but I can tell you've really caught feelings. I don't know Jake at all, but I have seen you with Fitz, and let me tell you – it's fire," Jules said pointedly.

"Yeah, not helping so much," Gabby laughed.

They stopped at the Bavarian Glass Art booth where Gabby purchased two beautiful hand-blown glass ornaments for her parents: a snowman and a Santa. She figured they could hang them from the rearview mirror during the holidays, if they went through with buying an RV.

She also bought an angel for herself. Its face was nondescript with blonde glass for hair, a blue dress with white swirls, and beautiful white angel wings. Gabby could not wait to hang it on her little tree back at her apartment.

Christmas was in two weeks, and she loved to decorate and transform her apartment. She put on an old Johnny Mathis Christmas album that her dad used to play throughout the holidays when she was little. It truly was amazing how scent and music could call up a memory in an instant.

Gabby loved to melt cinnamon wax melts throughout her place, along with other holiday scents. Her five-foot frosted spruce tree with white lights sat in the corner of her living room next to her chaise couch. She was excited to host her parents for Christmas in the city for the very first time, so she wanted to make it extra special. Along with placing single battery powered candles in her bedroom window and her living room window, she had hung garland from her kitchen peninsula and tied into it Christmas knickknacks she had collected while thrifting.

Gabby even had a special menu planned. She had been looking through the recipe box that her mom gave her at Thanksgiving. She planned to try her hand at several of the recipes.

At Syrin – Handmade Slavic gifts, Gabby bought her mom a nesting doll set that looked like five snowmen. Each looked like the other but had different colored hats and scarves of reds and blues and, of course, nested in one another. They were also handmade in Russia. Gabby's parents loved culture and loved to travel. As a child, since her parents were off all summer from their job as teachers, Gabby was able to travel to so many amazing places. She just knew her mom would love the gift.

"One of these booths has these really cool German beer steins. I want to find one for my dad," Gabby said to Jules.

As they rounded the corner, she stopped abruptly. There was Jake with his arm around some girl looking at ornaments up ahead. He leaned down and kissed her intimately. The girl wrapped her arms around his waist in a hug. Gabby felt like she had been punched in the gut.

"I think the booth you are looking for is right around the corner," Jules said.

Her voice trailed off as she followed Gabby's gaze just in time to see Jake grab the girl's face and kiss her.

"Is that ...?"

"Jake."

"Come on, let's get out of here. We can come back for the beer stein another day, right?" Jules linked arms with Gabby to try to steer her in the opposite direction.

"No. No. It's fine. We weren't exclusive. He can date whomever he wants to. Right? Right? And it's not like I haven't been talking to Fitz. It's fine. I will say hi. No, I better not. Ugh. Why is this so difficult?"

"Gabby, you're spiraling."

Before Gabby and Jules could pivot, Gabby heard her name, and she knew the voice all too well.

"Gabby! Wait up!"

Gabby spun around slowly and forced a smile on her face.

"Hey … you …" She gave Jake a brief side hug.

Jake introduced Gabby to What's-her-face. What's-her-face said hello and shook Gabby's hand. It was so awkward. What bothered her the most was that the entire exchange did not seem as awkward for Jake. Let's be real – she hadn't seen him since Thanksgiving, despite some texts back and forth. What did she expect? Maybe the decision had been made for her.

"Well, it's cold. And I'm trying to finish up some Christmas shopping. The big day is coming soon. Big Day. Christmas. Nice to see you, Jake. Nice to meet you …" She drifted off and silently thought *What's-your-face*.

Gabby turned and briskly walked quickly in the opposite direction. She didn't know where she was headed as long as it was far away from whatever that just was.

"Gabby! Whoa, wait up!" Jules called after her.

Gabby finally stopped fast-walking when she reached the entrance of the market. She bent over with her hands on her knees.

"I am not built for this. I don't run. I need to get out of here. I just want to go home."

"I'm parked across the street in the parking garage. I will drive you back to your apartment."

Gabby and Jules rode in silence back to River North. After Gabby let herself into her apartment, she kicked off her shoes, dropped her purse and coat by the door, put her purchases away, and crawled right into bed.

And cried herself to sleep.

Chapter Eighteen

Gabby woke up to several missed text messages from Jake.

Gabby, I'm sorry. It's not really what you think.

Gabby, please, we need to talk.

Gabby, I know you're upset. I know you. Please just text me or call me when you're ready.

And from Jules. *Hey girl. Just checking in. I told Mack you stayed home sick. Just text me when you feel like it.*

Gabby didn't want to wallow. She had done plenty of that in her younger years. Was she hurt? Of course, she was. She wasn't ready to face Jake or speak to him anytime soon. And at the end of the day, Jake didn't do anything wrong. So why was she so upset? What Gabby did was put up her little wall and leave it like that. It was her solution for the time being.

Bartleby would not leave Gabby alone until she went into the kitchen and fed him. Mr. B. was a tabby cat with beautiful gold eyes. It didn't matter if he had half the bowl full. He was not happy until the bowl was filled to the brim.

"My liege," Gabby said as she bowed down dramatically and set his bowl in front of him.

Gabby padded over to the couch, grabbed the remote and a blanket, and turned on the TV. *If I'm playing hooky, might as well make it a good, lazy day.*

Gabby put her phone on "do not disturb" after she had a Starbucks Venti Caramel Ribbon Crunch Frap delivered to her door and proceeded to binge watch comedies and thrillers on Netflix. Being disconnected from the world was kind of blissful. Peace and quiet and self-reflection were just what Gabby needed. She never called in sick, so she didn't even feel guilty about taking a mental health day.

After a few hours of television, Gabby took a shower and decided to go to an exhibit she had wanted to check out at the Art Institute of Chicago. The exhibit was called *THINKING OF ~~YOU.~~ I MEAN ~~ME~~. I MEAN YOU* by Barbara Kruger. The short of it was an installation combining images with text, using humor and empathy, to expose power dynamics of consumerism and desire. Gabby could not think of a better way to shut her brain down than with a walk through her favorite art museum and her phone on silent. She loved immersive installations such as Kruger's.

One of the first exhibits displayed a photo that read, "iPhone therefore I am." Gabby hated the dependency on phones and the need for constant gratification, even though it was definitely one of her flaws. She hated waiting for others and had zero patience. Which made her think about making Fitz and Jake wait on her.

Food for thought. There is something to be said for being more meaningful and present as well, she mused.

Gabby read aloud, "You are what you think you are and your body is a battleground."

She thought back to her teenage years. She was very shy, naïve, and always the jokester. Gabby didn't have a lot of self-esteem at that time. But Jake didn't care. He loved her for who she was. And she had come a long way in the confidence department.

The exhibit transcended the entire museum, which was really fascinating. Why do we allow others to dictate our self-worth? The introspection forced Gabby to revisit some of the dates she had in the prior months.

"Today is the first day of the rest of your life," Gabby read the literal writing on the wall.

Well, I guess we will see.

And with that, Gabby left the museum and headed back to her place.

Gabby stepped off the elevator and started to walk to her apartment when she saw Jake sitting on the floor with his back against the wall next to her door. He looked pitiful. As soon as Jake saw Gabby, he hopped up quickly.

"Gabby …"

She opened her apartment door and set her purse down on the entrance table and picked up the cat as she walked over to her sofa. Jake followed her into the apartment.

"I don't even know what to say. I never meant to hurt you."

"Jake, stop. Honestly. You did nothing wrong. At no point did we ever say we were exclusive. It was just a shock to see you with someone else. It was weird for me because you will always have a piece of my heart."

"It's not really serious with her. But I kind of want to also see where it goes."

"And you should. Don't let this," Gabby waved her hand in the air, "whatever we are or were, stop you from that."

"I need to get going, but I couldn't leave things that way. Not with you."

"We're good. I am fine. Everything is fine."

Gabby walked Jake to the door, and he gave her a big hug. He whispered, "You will always be my girl next door."

She squeezed him back. Inside she felt so sad and hollow. She couldn't put it into words.

After Jake left, Gabby didn't know how to feel. She was definitely sad but also a tiny bit relieved in a way. And she wanted Jake to be happy. She was also confident he would want the same for her.

Gabby turned her phone back on and called her mom, who told her the house sold. Gabby winced at the news but pushed through to discuss their upcoming plans for Christmas.

"You and Dad can have my bed. I will sleep on the couch. It's actually super comfy."

"But how will Santa deliver the presents if you are sleeping next to the tree?" Gabby's mom asked her.

"Cute, Mom. I hope you guys are excited. Because I am to have you here."

"We are, honey. Talk soon! I love you, Gabriella."

"Love you too, Mom."

She called Jules next to fill her in. Then Gabby noticed she had a text from Fitz:

F: *After my practice tomorrow, how about I grab a quick shower and you meet me at the rink for a skate?*

G: *Sorry, I just saw your message. I don't know how to ice skate.*

F: *It's okay. I got you! Just meet me. Please.*

G: *Okay. Text me the time to be there and I will come over from my office.*

F: *Can't wait ;)*

Gabby couldn't help but smile. She was actually excited to go to work tomorrow because she was excited to see Fitz. She had not seen him in person since the club. Thinking about him gave her

major butterflies.

Chapter Nineteen

The next evening after work, Gabby met Fitz at the rink where the Blackhawks played. Fitz looked so cute in his Blackhawks beanie. He could make anything look good. Gabby noticed that when he smiled, he had a dimple on his right cheek. And of course, he smelled amazing, which Gabby noticed when he hugged her hello. She could get used to wrapping her arms around his waist. Fitz picked her up mid-hug, and Gabby laughed.

They had the rink to themselves. Gabby guessed he had the ability to pull those kinds of strings. It felt like their own private event. She looked around at the vast expanse of seats around the ice rink. Gabby had never seen it empty like that. Whenever she was there, for work mainly, the place was packed with fans. She felt really special to be there with Fitz.

They sat on the Blackhawks bench, and Fitz helped Gabby lace up her skates, then helped her onto the ice. At first Gabby held onto the boards for dear life and took baby steps along the rink. A few times she wobbled enough to nearly fall, but Fitz caught her every time. Eventually, she shuffled forward without holding onto the boards, and Fitz held her hand. At times he also put his hands on her waist or the small of her back. When he did that, it sent chills down her spine because she could feel his breath on the back of her neck. Her mind flashed back to when they danced at the club.

On cue, Fitz had Gabby pinned against the boards and bent down to kiss her. She loved how tall he was, especially on skates. It made Gabby feel safe and secure. She kissed him back. Hard. Gabby wanted to make it very clear to Fitz how she felt.

They sat on the bench and took a break. Gabby took off her gloves, and Fitz put her hands in his and blew on them and tried to warm them up. He was so sweet and kept finding ways to physically touch her. He kept asking her questions about her childhood and upbringing.

Gabby asked him, "I want to know more about you. Where did you grow up?"

"I grew up in a relatively poor neighborhood on the south side of Chicago. My dad split when my brothers and I were very young, and my mom worked two jobs to support us. I really lucked out by having a place to go and stay out of trouble. The Kroc Stadium was a place my brothers and I went to after school and played sports. I was fortunate to find a coach who introduced me to hockey at a young age. Lots of donated equipment and inner-city hockey practices until I was old enough to work to buy some nicer equipment and pay for ice time. Thankfully a practicing travel team kept noticing me at the rink and … the rest is history. Getting drafted by the Hawks in my hometown was a dream come true."

"Wow. I have so much respect for your mom and what she had to do to raise you guys. I'm sure it was not easy."

"We were a handful. Landon is my older brother, and he is a psychologist. My younger brother, Logan, is in college studying sports medicine."

"She must be very proud of you three. Amazing. My parents both just retired and sold my childhood home. They plan on traveling. I was devastated at first, but they have worked so hard for what they have. They deserve to travel and live their lives."

Fitz abruptly got up and walked to the end of the bench. He returned with a thermos and mugs.

"What have you got there?" Gabby asked with a wink.

"I completely forgot. Hot cider!"

He poured out two mugs of hot apple cider. Gabby blew on her mug and felt the warmth enter her hands and spread throughout her body. She took a sip. It was absolutely perfect.

"How on earth did you do this when you had practice?"

"Oh, I have my ways."

"I have no doubt about that. I am very interested in learning what all those ways are."

"Oh yeah?" Fitz bumped into her playfully. "By the way, I have some road games coming up on the west coast. I would love to call you from the road, if that's ok. Not just text. I want to be able to hear your voice."

"I would love that."

After a few more trips around the rink, Gabby and Fitz took off their skates and he walked Gabby to her car.

"I will text *and* call you from the road."

"I am counting on it."

Fitz gave Gabby a sweet kiss and closed her car door. Gabby put her heat on as high as it could go *and* her heated seat. She was cold from the rink, but her face was also flushed from the kiss.

She smiled all the way to her apartment.

Chapter Twenty

Gabby was putting cheese and crackers onto a little board when she heard a knock at her apartment door. She peeked through the peep hole to see Jules standing there.

"Hey!! I have snacks and wine! Not sure if it's "hockey watching food," but I hope you are hungry."

"I could eat," Jules said. "Oooh… a 'coochie' board! Fancy."

Gabby laughed as she said, "Here, can you grab this bowl of dip for me?

Jules and Gabby took the drinks and food into the living room. They were getting ready to watch the Chicago Blackhawks at the Anaheim Ducks.

"I actually feel kind of nervous," Gabby said. "It's so different knowing someone who has a stake in the game. And to be honest, I actually miss him. Our skating date the other night was perfect."

"Not gonna lie, you look really happy," Jules said.

"And what about you? How's Trevor?"

"Oh, Trevor is old news. I'm just swiping left and right whenever I feel like it," Jules laughed.

Already? Gabby thought, then said, "Oh my god, I am glad you said that! You reminded me to delete that dating app. Fitz and I haven't had a talk about the status of our relationship, but I do know I am not interested in spending time with anyone else."

"That is really huge news! I am truly happy for you," Jules said.

The announcer said the puck was about to drop. The game was so fast paced. Gabby had a hard time watching where the puck was going. And she was not a fan of people getting slammed into the boards.

"Can you believe that Fitz had me skating around on the ice? Thank God he was there to hold me up."

All of a sudden, the girls heard, "GOAALLLLL!!!! Lucas Fitzgerald with the top shelf one-timer!! That's where grandma keeps the good stuff!"

Gabby and Jules both jumped up and high-fived each other.

"That's my man!" Gabby yelled.

Jules said, "He's a good stick handler. Imagine what else he can do with ..."

Before Jules could finish her sentence, Gabby snorted and spit wine all over the coffee table. She walked over to the kitchen to get paper towels to clean up the mess. While she was in the kitchen, Gabby refilled their snacks and drinks.

She heard Jules shout, "Gabby, you need to come back in here!"

As Gabby walked back into the living room, she heard the announcer say, "Lucas Fitzgerald with a nasty hit from behind that sent him into the boards. It's times like this you pray his family isn't watching."

The sports channel kept playing the hit over and over again while the medics loaded Fitz onto a stretcher.

"Oh god. Is that blood? Is that blood on the ice? I think I'm going to be sick." Gabby turned off the game, and Jules hugged her tightly.

Gabby tried both calling Fitz and texting him, but it kept going to voicemail. Which she figured. But she had to at least try.

Jules watched Gabby pace until midnight, then went home after sending Gabby to bed. Gabby could barely sleep and tossed and turned most of the night. Finally, about 4:00 a.m. Chicago time, her cell phone rang.

"Hello?" Gabby answered on the first ring.

"Hey, Ticket Sales."

"Oh my goodness. You had me so worried!! Are you okay? That was a nasty hit."

Fitz said, "I am under concussion protocol, but otherwise I will be okay. They're releasing me from the hospital in time to fly home with the team. How about that goal though?"

"You hockey players! How many hits to the head have you had in your career?" Gabby asked.

"This was the first really bad hit I have taken. Listen, I would like to see you when we land. Like, I NEED to see you. Can you meet me at the airport?"

Gabby smiled. "I think I can do that for you, *Top Shelf*."

The next day, Gabby drove Jules insane pacing and trying to pass the time. It felt like the longest day ever!

"Well, at least you are getting your steps in," Jules joked.

"I *need* to see him. I need to tell him how I feel," Gabby.

Jules agreed to drive to the airport with Gabby to keep her company and *in her words* to, "scope out the hot hockey players." She appreciated the company and support from her regardless. *Jules is a solid friend. One of the best. I need to tell her that as well. When you feel something, you should just say it! Don't let the moment pass you by.*

Gabby and Jules arrived the following evening on the tarmac at O'Hare Airport. Mack had somehow hooked them up with special clearance to be able to greet the team as they deplaned. Gabby paced and paced and didn't notice how chilly it was. She was nervous. The team plane had landed, and she was impatiently waiting for them to disembark.

Finally, the team came down the stairs, and Gabby anxiously looked for Fitz. She finally spotted him and ran over, security be damned. Gabby jumped up and wrapped her legs around his waist and kissed him.

"Oh shoot! Your head. I'm so sorry! How are you feeling? I am so glad you're okay. But I'm not sure I can handle being a hockey girlfriend. I was so worried about you."

"Oh, is that what you are now?" Fitz smirked.

"Is that all you heard?" Gabby rolled her eyes.

"I can't promise I will never get hurt again. But I can promise I will never hurt you. Gabby, you're it for me. Spending time with you, getting injured, being away from you … It really put some things into perspective for me. I am all in. If you'll have me."

"I believe you. I really do. You don't just tell me how you feel, your actions show me how much you really care. I am all in with you."

"I hope I have the chance to show you how much you mean to me for a long time. I love you, you know."

Gabby grinned as she remembered the note on the back of one of her grandmother's recipes.

Before she could return his words, Fitz leaned in and she eagerly welcomed his kiss. They stood on the tarmac wrapped in each other while people moved around them, like they were the only ones in the world.

This is it, Gabby thought as Fitz's lips moved against hers. She could feel it in her bones. *After these last few crazy months, everything I was looking for found me on its own time. This is my happily ever*

after. This is the good stuff.

THE END

Acknowledgments

To my family: husband, Chris; children, Kali, Dylan, Carson, Jace, Dominick, and Aiden (and Cody): The unwavering support when I was writing and editing, the cheers and encouragement means the world to me. Lukas – we miss you.

Mom and Dad: Thomas and Laura Temple thank you for always having my back and loving and supporting me. There was nothing that I felt I could not do with you behind me.

My siblings: Tommy, Matthew, Kailey, Jen, and Jay thank you for being in my corner. I love you all!

Kaitlyn, David, Ezra, Isaiah, and Toby: Life is better with you in it. Always know how much I love you!

Mom and Dad Turner: I have always felt welcomed, supported, and loved. I am so grateful.

My besties and soul sisters: Lisa, Drianna, Lynda, Christina, Sabrina, Rachelle, Kelly, Jennifer, Stacie, Sarah, and Tara: Decades of friendship… what a pleasure it is to have you all as friends. Thank you for all the love and support.

Kimberly and Lyndsay: There is not enough space here to thank you for the years and years of support no matter what journey I am on. You both have ALWAYS been there for me and my family. I am so grateful to you.

The best editor and friend: Sara Butka, (Sara Mack – Author): Thank you for taking on my project. I have learned so much from you and the contributions you made to this project means the world to me. It has been an honor to have one of my own favorite authors mentor me.

Thank you to the masses who contributed their bad date stories to me, or beta read my story and provided feedback.

Lastly, if you think that one of the situations could be written about you – it is probably just a coincidence.

Made in the USA
Columbia, SC
15 February 2024

31652916R00117